Beneath My Mother's Feet

· AMJED QAMAR ·

ATHENEUM BOOKS FOR YOUNG READERS
NEW YORK   LONDON   TORONTO   SYDNEY

ATHENEUM BOOKS FOR YOUNG READERS

An imprint of Simon & Schuster Children's Publishing Division

1230 Avenue of the Americas, New York, New York 10020

For information about special discounts for bulk purchases, please contact

Simon & Schuster Special Sales at 1-866-506-1949 or business@simonandschuster.com.

The Simon & Schuster Speakers Bureau can bring authors to your live event. For more information or to book an event, contact the Simon & Schuster Speakers Bureau at 1-866-248-3049 or visit our website at www.simonspeakers.com.

Also available in an Atheneum Books for Young Readers hardcover edition.

Book design by Michael McCartney

The text for this book is set in Perpetua Standard.

Manufactured in the United States of America

First Atheneum Books for Young Readers paperback edition April 2011

10 9 8 7 6 5 4 3 2 1

The Library of Congress has cataloged the hardcover edition as follows:

Qamar, Amjed

Beneath my mother's feet / Amjed Qamar.— 1st ed.

p. cm

Summary: When her father is injured, fourteen-year-old Nazia is pulled away from school, her friends, and her preparations for an arranged marriage, to help her mother clean houses in a wealthy part of Karachi, Pakistan, where she finally rebels against the destiny that is planned for her.

ISBN 978-1-4169-4728-8 (hc)

[1. Family life—Pakistan—Fiction. 2. Household employees—Fiction. 3. Pakistan—Fiction. 4. Self-actualization (Psychology)—Fiction. 5. Sex role—Fiction. 6. Poverty—Fiction.] 1. Title.

PZ7.Q13Be 2008

[Fic]—dc22

2007019001

ISBN 978-1-4424-1451-8 (pbk)

ISBN 978-1-4424-0705-3 (eBook)

Acknowledgments

In loving memory of Ammijan (my courageous
mother-in-law), Dadajan (my brilliant
father-in-law), and Munir (beloved little brother,
an angel among us). We miss you so much.

Thank you to all my friends who offered their
support and enthusiasm during this entire process.
From start to finish, you've made it fun.

And finally, I dedicate this book to my family,
especially Mom, my siblings, my children,
and to Adnan, who is everything.

———◂—

The musky scent of mustard oil intensified in the early-August heat. Nazia ran a hand across her tightly braided hair, then wiped the oil on the front of her rumpled *kameeze*. A yellowish-orange stain seeped into the cotton fabric of her shirt, and she regretted it immediately. Less than a week into the new school year, and already her starched white uniform was permanently stained. She grabbed a handful of sand from the side of the road and rubbed it in, hoping the earth would soak up at least some of the dense oil and save her from Amma's scolding.

She stood at the edge of the Gizri cloth bazaar, the afternoon sun pressing against her bare arms, face, and neck. Her house was in view just across the street, past the cricket pitch where a group of boys ran back and forth between the wickets, stirring up the dust. The bazaar was on the outskirts of Gizri colony, a working-class neighborhood in southern Karachi, and just a few kilometers from the Arabian Sea. Because the bazaar was two blocks long and adjacent to the Gizri School for Girls, it was nearly impossible to walk by day after day without getting drawn in by the enticing apparel.

Maleeha and Saira moved from stall to stall, tugging at silks and chiffons that fluttered from overhanging displays. Nazia shuffled along behind them and turned her gaze toward the main road that separated the bazaar from the cricket field. Beyond the steady rumble of cars, bicycles, buses, rickshaws, trucks, taxis, and the slower animal-drawn vehicles, the fielders scrambled forward to catch a high ball, their bare hands cupped together to ease the impact. She sighed when Maleeha called out to her. Why couldn't she be the batsman on the cricket pitch, poised for the bowler's next pitch, instead of looking at clothes she couldn't afford?

"This one." Maleeha unraveled a bolt of cloth and held a corner of the sheer material in the air. The gold brocade shimmered against the pink chiffon. "It's perfect for your *jahez*."

Nazia wrinkled her nose. "Amma could dress the entire school with the all the clothes she's made for my dowry. We don't need to add another." The strap of her backpack cut into her shoulder. She winced and shifted the weight to the other side. "Come on. I have to get home or Amma will be worried." She turned back toward the busy road and began walking.

"You're always so afraid of your mother," Saira complained.

"She's not afraid," Maleeha said. "She's just a good *beti*, a dutiful daughter."

Nazia lifted her chin higher and quickened her pace to escape their playful jabs. She'd known the two girls since Montessori; she knew their lives were no different from hers.

Maleeha dropped the cloth onto the cart and followed Nazia to the main road. The stall owner wrapped the material back into place.

"Once you get married, it won't matter anymore what color

you like. Your mother decides now, and when you get married, your mother-in-law will take her place." Maleeha looked pointedly at Nazia but kept walking. "And you, Nazia, will agree to everything. Just like you always do."

Nazia looked at her friend sharply. "You know that'll never change. Our lives will always be in the hands of our mothers, whether we like it or not."

Saira hurried to keep pace with them, her schoolbag constantly falling off her thick shoulders. "My mother always says that you can eat whatever you like, but you have to wear what others choose."

Maleeha snorted. "You eat everything in sight."

Nazia remained silent, having heard the same words from her own mother time and again. She stopped at the edge of the street, squinting to avoid the flashy sunlight that bounced from car to car. She waited for an opening to cross. The street was teeming with Suzuki trucks, compact cars, and ornately decorated buses. An occasional *tonga* clattered by, the driver and his passenger perched atop the two-wheeled wooden cart pulled by a donkey daring enough to brave the traffic. The day's pollution had settled, and a haze hung over the city. Nazia pulled out a scarf from her backpack—the *dupatta* that should have been on her head—and pressed it against her face to keep from breathing in the exhaust fumes.

When she saw an opening, she clutched her backpack and dashed across the street, jumping over the median to the other side. "Come on!" She looked back to make sure her friends had made it, then headed down the street that ran alongside the cricket field.

A horn blasted loudly behind her, and she jerked to the right.
A truck rumbled past, the flatbed crammed with men, their
bodies jostling as the truck sped over bumps and craters in the
unpaved road. She spotted her father. What was he doing home at
this time of day? He was half sitting, half lying down. It seemed
as though the men were cradling his body. The truck sped on,
leaving behind a cloud of dust.

She broke into a run, her bag bouncing against her back.
Maleeha and Saira scrambled to keep up. The game of cricket
stopped, and Nazia knew that the players were wondering if one
of their fathers was on the truck.

By the time Nazia reached the house, Abbu was already inside.
Maleeha and Saira came in behind her, panting heavily. Nazia
moved behind the men gathered around her parents' mattress on
the floor of the cramped room, where her father lay. She stepped
in closer and wrinkled her nose at the stench of their sweat. Their
clothes were covered with dirt, their thick hair matted. She
cupped a hand over her nose and watched two men adjust the
cushions around Abbu in an attempt to make him comfortable.
But she knew, from the way her father clenched his teeth and kept
his eyes squeezed shut, that comfort was far off.

His left arm was wrapped in a scrap of cloth, leaving his wrist
hanging limp. A bandage covered his left leg from foot to mid
thigh. The white gauze was smeared with dirt, and large patches
of blood seeped through, glistening wet.

He must have gotten injured at work. Abbu was a construction worker at a building site just outside Karachi. He never came home before dark and often stayed overnight guarding the machinery whenever there was a strike or curfew. After losing his previous job a few weeks earlier, Abbu had moved around several times before settling with this one.

Isha and Mateen were on the floor beside Abbu clutching his soiled *kurta*. Their small hands were indifferent to the mud smeared all over his long shirt. Nazia wanted to push her way past the men to sit beside her younger brother and sister, but she felt too old to cry with everyone watching. Just then Amma bustled forward carrying a pitcher of water and a glass. She called Nazia to the front.

Amma's mouth was a firm line, but her eyes were round and watery. "Hold the tray so the men can drink." Before Nazia could reply, Amma shoved the tray into her hands and then knelt beside Abbu, speaking words in a whisper too soft to hear.

Nazia shuffled through the crowd with the tray, eyes cast downward, as each man turned away from her father and drank warm water from the glass. She could feel their gaze on the top of her head, and some men passed a hand over her hair, blessing her as if she were their daughter.

Later she heard the men explain to Amma that bricks from a new section had fallen from the building under construction. Abbu had been leaning against a high wall, believing the cement had hardened. The cement was tainted, though, and the shaky structure had given way, crumbling onto him. Pieces of concrete had fallen on his leg and some on his arm. It would be months before Abbu could work again.

———— ► ————

Three weeks later Nazia was bent over her school desk, her stomach grumbling as she struggled to finish her assignment. She felt a sharp jab in her back and turned swiftly to glare at Maleeha. "Stop it!"

"Well, if you don't hurry up, we're going to eat our lunch without you." Maleeha nodded toward Saira, who was just turning in her paper to their teacher, Ms. Haroon.

"Go on, then," Nazia said. She gripped her pencil tighter. The assignment was based on last night's reading about Quaid-i-Azam Mohammad Ali Jinnah, the founder of Pakistan, but Nazia had been so busy helping her mother that she had been too tired to do her homework. She pressed a fist against her stomach to quiet the gurgling.

Since Abbu's accident they had gotten by with money Amma had tucked away from her sewing. In the first week neighbors had brought bowls of curried *daal*, *samosas*, and boiled rice. Now the pantry was nearly bare but for the half-empty tin of flour and the square bucket that held broken—nearly crushed—grains of rice. Even the daal consisted of yellow lentils watered down to stretch through the week.

Amma had counted on Bilal finding work, but Nazia's older brother had done what he always did when the family needed him—he had disappeared. At sixteen, he'd completed his diploma last spring, and now he spent his days roaming the vast city with friends instead of going on to college. He often disappeared for days at a stretch, claiming to be looking for work. None of his excuses ever made sense, but somehow the teasing way he said it, and the gifts he brought home when he returned, made the stories irrelevant to Nazia. When Bilal *bhai* was home, she could be a little sister again. Only this time he hadn't come back.

Maleeha nudged her shoulder. "Just write anything! You're Ms. Haroon's favorite — you know she'd never fail you anyway."

The sharp click of heels echoed down the hall outside the classroom. "Uh-oh," Maleeha said, and slid back into her seat.

Ms. Haroon snapped her fingers. "Everyone in your seats quickly." She took her dupatta from behind her chair and draped the lengthy scarf over her shoulders.

By the time Madam Qureshi arrived, the room was silent but for the whir of the overhead fan. The class greeted the principal by belting out "Good afternoon, Madam Qureshi" in unison. She gave an almost imperceptible nod of her head before whispering something to Ms. Haroon.

Nazia stiffened as her teacher stared at her, all the while nodding solemnly. Was she in trouble? This wasn't the first time she hadn't done her homework. But the principal knew about her father's accident. Knew that there was little time after school to study. She had kept up as best she could, and unlike Bilal bhai, she found schoolwork came naturally to her. Except when she didn't do her homework.

Ms. Haroon called her name and motioned her forward. Maleeha's finger dug into her back, and her singsong voice taunted, "Nazia's in trouble."

"You are such a baby," Nazia muttered. She stood up, pushed in her chair, and strode to the front of the class, feeling all eyes upon her. *It's nothing,* she told herself. *Just tell them you'll make up the assignments and take on extra work to keep up with the class.* Since it was only a month into the school year, the assignments were still fairly light.

"Yes?" Nazia stood with her hands clasped behind her back, trying hard not to crack her fingers so the other students couldn't see how nervous she was.

"Your mother is here. She is withdrawing you for the day." Madam Qureshi peered at Nazia. "Is everything okay at home? Is your father better?"

From the corner of her eye Nazia saw the first row of students lean forward. Why was everyone so nosey about her father? *A wall fell on him,* she wanted to shout. "Abbu is still in bandages," she mumbled instead. "Not the same ones," she added. "Amma changes them every day." The principal and teacher stared at her. She felt her classmates staring, and all the eyes bored into her flesh. "We have to change them every day so his wounds don't get infected."

"Well," Madam Qureshi said with a sigh. "Gather your things. Your mother is waiting."

Nazia turned to her teacher. "What about my assignment? I'm not finished."

Ms. Haroon smiled. "It's all right. I'll take what you have."

Nazia's throat constricted. "But I could take it home and bring it tomorrow." She was trying to keep the whine out of her voice.

"No, *beta.* There's no need for that. I'll take it as it is." Ms. Haroon rubbed the sweat off her face with the corner of her dupatta. Even with the fan, the room was unbearably hot.

Why had Amma come? She never came to the school, and

now it meant that Nazia would fall even more behind. She could always get the next assignment later from Maleeha or Saira, but she had no idea when she'd find the time to finish it.

She went back to her desk and began shoving books inside her bag.

"Where are you going?" Maleeha whispered.

Nazia shrugged. "My mother's here. I have to go."

"Do you think something happened to your *abbu?*"

Nazia grabbed the unfinished assignment on her desk and shook her head. "No. He's much better now. He just can't work yet." She looked over at Saira and waved good-bye. "Maybe I'll see you later tonight. We can play cricket."

Maleeha wrinkled her nose. "I'm not playing cricket," she half yelled, half whispered.

Nazia hurried to catch up with Madam Qureshi, who was already clicking her way down the hall.

"Amma! Wait for us!" Nazia called as she jumped down from the bus that had brought them from the Gizri School for Girls to the Defence Market. The market was a sprawling cluster of upscale shops just on the outskirts of the Defence Housing Society, a section of residential homes for Karachi's elite.

Nazia was always awed by the transformation that occurred as they moved away from the narrow, trash-filled streets of the housing developments behind the Gizri commercial area toward the palatial mansions that lined the main thoroughfare when they entered the upper-class housing society.

The Defence commercial area sat at the base of Phase 5, the section known for its lavish homes and proximity to the Arabian Sea. The buses never went into the residential streets, so outsiders had to walk through the commercial market, where tailors, toy shops, bookstores, meat stalls, restaurants, and bakeries catered to the wealthy. Here the upper class bought their goods, rather than having to brave the inner city of Karachi.

Defence was, for all practical purposes, a self-contained city for the elite socialites to shop at the trendiest stores, eat at the best restaurants, and have their hair and makeup done at beauty salons owned by celebrities featured on Pakistan Television.

Nazia helped Isha and Mateen off the bus and herded them toward Amma, who was already far ahead, walking purposefully toward a thin woman standing in front of a meat shop.

Slabs of meat hung from metal hooks at the open-air shop. Whole chickens, plucked and skinned, were strung from a bar and dangled upside down by a single limb. The butcher swatted lazily at the dense layer of flies, but it was a useless gesture. The flies rose up in flight, only to return and settle immediately on the slabs of warm meat.

"Amma, what are we doing here?" Amma refused to offer any information. All she'd said at school was that she had something important to do, and Nazia was to watch Isha and Mateen while she did it.

"This is your daughter?" The woman at the shop smiled at Amma. She wore jewelry that clinked and sparkled with her every movement, drawing attention from the crowd of men around the stall. Her dupatta was draped casually over her head and slipped back farther every time she moved. Her body seemed to dance in waves, even though her feet were planted firmly on the ground. Her clothes were worn, and her face had the weathered look of someone who spent day after day toiling under the sun.

Amma wiped her round face with the corner of her dupatta. Sweat dripped down her neck and plastered the front of her kameeze to her chest. "Yes. Nazia is fourteen. She'll be married at the end of the school year. Isha is ten and Mateen is four." Amma nudged Nazia forward. "Where are your manners? Say *salaam* to Shenaz!"

Nazia mumbled a greeting and turned back to Amma. "What are we doing here?"

"Your mother is here to find work," Shenaz said.

"But she is working. She sews clothes."

"It's not enough, beta." Shenaz looked at Nazia with soft eyes. "Your big brother has run away, and your father is taking his time recovering from his injury."

"He broke his leg." Who did this woman think she was, accusing Abbu like that? Injuries like his took time.

"It's been weeks, child. How do you expect to get married if there's no money to pay for your jahez? There is so much to manage far before the wedding day."

"It's not just your wedding, Nazia." Amma's voice was weary. "What about the rent? Neighbors bringing food is fine for a while. The sewing covers the small necessities, but we have to find a way to pay for the roof over our heads."

Nazia thought. There had to be another way. Then her eyes

brightened. "I know! Why don't you ask Uncle Tariq? You know he will do anything to help us."

Amma pursed her lips and shook her head.

"But why not?" Nazia frowned.

"You know why. You will marry his son soon. We cannot humiliate ourselves in front of him before the wedding! He cannot know of our hardships."

"But why not? If they are willing to have me in their family, then taking care of us for a few months before should not matter."

"Even we have our pride, Nazia. We may not have much more than that, but at least we have our pride."

What good is pride if it just gets in the way? Nazia stared at Amma. Was there no other way? Were they really that poor? She had always believed that they were well off, that money would never be an issue. Whenever anyone in the neighborhood had troubles, Amma was among the first to share whatever they had in the house. "What kind of work?" she asked finally.

"I've set up some houses for your mother," Shenaz said as she began walking past the shops toward the hill, where the homes were larger than any Nazia had ever seen. "Come on — we have to move faster. If your mother does well, then the *memsahib* will keep her. I've got three houses waiting for her."

Amma's breath came in short gasps as she tried to keep up with Shenaz. "You'll need to watch over Isha and Mateen while I do the houses."

"Houses?" Nazia's cheeks grew warm. "You mean *clean* houses? Like a *masi*?"

"Yes," Amma grunted.

Nazia stopped short and gaped at her mother, who had never worked outside her home a day in her life. "Does Abbu know?"

"*Nahi*, of course not." Amma's panting grew more labored as she continued her climb.

"You haven't told him?" Nazia balled up her fists, nails digging into her palms. How could Amma make such a hasty decision without even checking with Abbu? Didn't she know how protective he was of their family? Did she think he would not mind? What would he say when he learned that Amma was shaming their family name and sullying Abbu's honor? What would he do when he found out? And then another thought occurred to her: If Amma intended to keep this from Abbu, why did she bring the children along? Did she really think they would not speak of it to their father?

"You want me to watch Isha and Mateen? Why didn't you just leave them at home with Abbu? Did you have to pull me out of school?" She was falling behind because she had to babysit?

Amma didn't look back. "Abbu wasn't home."

Nazia grabbed Mateen and slung him onto her hip as she hurried to keep up. "Not home? Amma, he can't walk."

Amma stopped abruptly and turned to Nazia. "Your abbu *can* walk. He limps, yes. His injuries were bad. Gashes and bruises, but no broken bones. His leg has healed. He goes to the market for most of the day while you are away at school. He comes home and lies in bed just before you return." She glanced at Mateen and moved on. "Ask your brother. He knows."

Nazia sucked in her breath and tightened her grip on Mateen. Why was Amma always seeing the worst in Abbu? Before the injury Abbu was gone every day, toiling from dawn to late in the night. How could someone like that bear the torture of lying motionless in bed for weeks?

Nazia could picture her father attempting to regain his strength as soon as she left for school each morning: Abbu lying on the mattress to exercise his leg as he lifted, pulled, and stretched. She knew that as soon as he was able, Abbu would urge his limbs to carry his weight and go back to work.

Mateen put a chubby hand on her cheek, turning her face toward him. "It's true." He pouted. "Abbu goes out all day, and he doesn't even play with me."

Nazia moved his hand away. "He can't play with you all the time. He needs to get better. He can't do that lying around the house, can he?"

There were times when the gaps between Abbu's paying jobs were long, but somehow they always managed to get by, and Abbu always found work again. Nazia decided that Amma was being too hard on him. Even if Abbu could walk, he was still far from recovered. He needed more time to heal before he could go back to doing construction work. And if he did go out, wasn't that the best way to work his leg and speed up his recovery? They couldn't afford to take him to a physiotherapist. Walking the market was the next best thing.

"Abbu knows what he is doing, Amma. You need to trust that he will take care of us like he always does. And when Abbu finds out about this, you know he'll be angry with you."

"Leave your mother alone," Shenaz called out. "She knows what is best for all of you."

Nazia glared at the woman's back, her flimsy clothes shifting with every step. "I'm only coming along for today," she shouted. "Don't expect us all to tag along tomorrow."

Shenaz was about to say something when Amma stopped her. "Leave her be. She will find out the truth soon enough."

There's nothing to find out, Nazia wanted to say. Amma should have stayed home and waited until he was better before going behind his back to find work. What was she thinking? Amma could easily have picked up some more clothes to sew or sold one or two pieces of jewelry set aside for the wedding. No matter what Shenaz said, there was still plenty of time to buy more for the jahez when Abbu found work again.

Nazia was still fuming when they turned onto a side street and stopped at a large teakwood gate. The house was surrounded by a tall concrete wall, with a row of coconut trees in wooden planters out front and a patch of lush green lawn that lined both sides of the gate. Shenaz spoke briefly with the gatekeeper while a uniformed guard stood watch under the shade of the palm leaves. He watched the group intently, one hand resting on the strap that held a rifle slung over his shoulder. The gatekeeper, a boy only a few years older than Nazia, disappeared behind the gate. He returned shortly and ushered them all inside.

When Nazia had passed the teakwood barrier, she nearly gasped at the beauty that lay hidden from the street. The front lawn was a deep shade of green, and the blades of grass were precisely trimmed. A rock formation covered a portion of the concrete wall, with water cascading from crevices. Nazia had seen one of these in a park once, but she'd had no idea that people built them in their own yards. Bougainvillea, roses, and jasmine filled the air with a heavy scent. Nazia and the children followed the women up the driveway and around to the side of the house, but Shenaz stopped and pulled Amma by the arm before they reached the door.

"Now remember, Naseem, the memsahib will ask you a few questions before she decides if she wants to hire you," Shenaz said. "Her name is Fatima and she sounds tough, but don't let her frighten you. Underneath she has a good heart — you'll see. She is always stern at first, because she just doesn't want anyone to take advantage of her." Shenaz snapped her fingers. "I almost forgot. Don't call her memsahib either. Just treat her like a big sister and call her *baji*. It's what most of these snooty women prefer to be called anyway."

Amma nodded, and they moved quickly to the kitchen door, where they were greeted by a tall, well-groomed woman. "Remove your shoes," she instructed.

Nazia knew the woman at the door must be Fatima, the memsahib of the house. She wore a brightly colored *shalwar* kameeze outfit made of starched lawn — a fine woven cotton that provided cool comfort in the sweltering heat. Nazia ran a hand across her own kameeze, the uniform suddenly unbearably heavy against her body.

She followed Amma into the house and set Mateen down onto the green marble floor next to Isha. It was deliciously cold, and she stepped slowly, savoring the sensation from heel to toe. They moved into a larger room, where the woman took a seat on the settee and motioned for everyone else to sit on the floor.

Shenaz plopped herself down at the woman's feet. Amma moved more slowly, settling gingerly on the floor. Nazia did the same, pulling her siblings close.

The woman studied Amma. "I am Fatima."

Amma nodded in greeting and offered her salaam.

"Have you cleaned houses before?"

Amma laughed. Her hands fluttered up and coaxed strands of limp hair back under the dupatta draped loosely over her head. "I know how to clean."

Fatima nodded. "My masi is expecting and cannot work anymore. She is sick all the time and bleeding. She's afraid she will lose the baby. So she left me." She leaned forward and narrowed her eyes. "You're not expecting, are you?"

Amma laughed some more and waved a hand at her children. "No, baji. See them? They are enough to keep an old woman like me spinning in circles."

Nazia felt the woman's eyes linger on her before her gaze moved back to Amma.

"Are you strong enough to do the work?" Fatima asked.

Shenaz's laughter interrupted the interrogation. "What kinds of questions are you asking, baji? You know women like us are strong enough to do the work of an ox." She patted Amma's thigh. "Naseem will do whatever you ask, and you will be happy with her work, you'll see." She winked at the memsahib. "Baji, have I ever brought you anyone who couldn't do the work?"

Fatima grimaced. "Yes, you have! Remember the *mali* who stole all my garden tools? The grass cutter, too. Now I make the gardeners bring their own supplies."

"Yes, one mistake," Shenaz agreed. "But only one. He was new from the village and didn't know better. If I ever see him again, I'll grab him by the ear and drag him to your feet for punishment."

"You'd better. My son sent those tools to me from America.

But it was my mistake. I shouldn't have given the tools to the gardener in the first place. My son was furious." Her eyes passed over Nazia. "Will your daughter be helping you?"

"Nahi, nahi, of course not," said Amma. "She is here only to watch the others. There was no place to leave the young ones."

"Make sure they stay on the veranda beside the kitchen. I don't want them all over the house. You people spread lice faster than flies on meat."

Fatima's words stung. Nazia's cheeks burned, and her throat ached as she swallowed the sharp words that boiled up inside her. She dipped her head quickly to glare at her toes. How dare this woman judge her! Nazia was meticulous with her combs, her oils, and the plaits of her braid. She'd never had lice in her life!

"Don't worry, baji, they will stay put," Amma mumbled.

"Okay, then. You can start by doing the dishes, then sweep the house and mop the floor. You will clean all the bathrooms, dust everything; then I have some laundry outside. When you've washed it, you can hang it to dry in back of the house." She stood up. "Go on now and get to work. Supplies are in the servant quarters behind the house. Shenaz, while you are here, could you mix the dough for the afternoon *roti*?"

"Yes, baji." Shenaz led the way out of the house, directed the children to sit on the veranda, and then took Amma to retrieve the supplies.

Nazia heard Shenaz coaching Amma as they walked away, telling her to be brave and not to dawdle. The baji hated when masis were slow. She wondered how Amma would be able to do all the work of the monstrous house alone. When she cleaned at home, Amma waddled from room to room at a slow and deliberate pace, never hurrying, never missing a spot. Even after caring for four children, her house, and Abbu, Amma didn't tire easily, but Nazia knew this job would be a near-impossible challenge for her mother.

While Amma cleaned and Shenaz kneaded dough, Nazia waited under the shade of the veranda, keeping Mateen and Isha occupied. The afternoon dragged and her stomach grumbled. She suddenly remembered that her lunch was still in her backpack, uneaten. She dug around in her bag and pulled out the smashed egg and roti sandwich Amma had made. Isha had eaten her flat-bread and egg sandwich on the bus but was still hungry. Nazia took a small bite and then gave the rest to Isha and Mateen. After the tiny morsel she felt even hungrier.

Over an hour later Shenaz came outside. She sighed heavily as she sat down beside Nazia. She inspected her bare feet, then picked calluses off her heels and scraped dirt from beneath her thick toenails. "Your mother is too slow." Shenaz's voice was sad. "Baji will never keep her at this rate."

Nazia cringed as she watched Shenaz pull off a strip of skin from her heel.

"Naseem says you are getting married soon. To your uncle's eldest son." Shenaz wiped her face with the bottom of her kameeze. The shirt was dingy and threadbare, and the outline of her body was visible when she tossed her dupatta on the floor and shook the collar of her shirt, fanning herself against the heat. The bangles on her wrist clinked together, but her chains were sweaty and stuck to her neck. "Have you met him?"

Nazia nodded. "Abbu arranged it when I was smaller, younger

than Mateen. Abbu was leaving the village to find work in Karachi. He came back for us later, but Uncle Tariq wanted us all to stay. He thought that if we went to the city, we would never come home again. So to keep the family peace, Abbu promised me in marriage to my cousin Salman."

Shenaz nodded. "That's how it's always done, beta. Have you seen him since then?"

"Three times? Maybe four. Abbu hasn't gone back to the village much." Nazia tried to picture her cousin, but his face was a hazy blur. "He's much older than me. Like a man now." To her the wedding day seemed very far off, and only since the talk lately about Abbu's job paying for the dowry did it suddenly seem closer than she expected. "Are you married?"

Shenaz threw her head back and laughed. "Of course — since I was a child like you. But he ran off with another *chokri*, a village girl. He comes back at times." She tapped her chest with a bony finger. "I have a soft heart and no children. So I let him stay awhile. When he leaves, sometimes I have money; sometimes he robs my cupboards clean. But I never mind, because I don't have to wake up to him every day. Now, the other woman" — she paused and wagged a finger at Nazia — "ahh, she gave him six sons and barely has the strength to leave her *charpai*."

Nazia's eyes widened. She couldn't imagine being so tired that she couldn't leave her bed.

Shenaz winked at her. "I have my strength and no one to tell me what to do except for the bajis. Not a bad life."

"But how do you feel safe at home, when your husband is gone?" Nazia asked.

"Ach. Everyone knows I am Abdullah's woman. No one would dare to enter my home. Besides, I live with my sister and her family; they are more than grateful for the money I share with them." Shenaz shrugged. "A small price to pay for protection, but at least I come and go as I please."

Nazia wondered what it would be like to have a husband who was rarely there. Never knowing when he was coming, sharing him with someone else, never knowing when he would bring gifts or steal your money. Most of all, she couldn't imagine any woman actually preferring to live that way. She'd been raised to believe that marriage was a fact of life, unchangeable, a destiny arranged by fathers, a tradition older than the land itself.

But she also knew that her teacher lived alone. And she was not so young either. How many times had she told the class about her travels up-country with only a tour guide from the British Arts Council and a group of Frenchmen on holiday? She never mentioned a family or children. But she talked incessantly about painting the craggy hills of Patriata or the ever-changing view from an air-conditioned railcar to Islamabad.

Nazia snuck another glance at Shenaz and decided that she might be proof that marriages don't always turn out the way a girl dreams. But Ms. Haroon? *She* was a book Nazia could read over and over and never tire of the tales stored up inside.

The screen door off the veranda banged open and Fatima stepped out, her hands on her hips, her face grim. "Shenaz! This woman is worthless. Half the day has gone by and she's just finishing the mopping!"

"Baji, your house is too big. There is so much to clean — it takes time." Shenaz kept her voice soft. "Give her a chance, baji. It's her first time."

"I'm not running a training center for masis." Fatima's voice rose. "I need the work finished now. The *sahib* is bringing guests shortly. How do you expect me to serve tea when the masi is still in the room dawdling on the floor?"

Nazia saw Mateen's lip tremble at the angry words, and she motioned for Isha to move closer to comfort their brother.

Fatima glared at Nazia. "What are you doing just sitting out here? I've had masis younger than you. Get up, child! Your sister can watch the baby." She held the screen door open. "Get in there and help your mother. Be quick about it, or you will not be back tomorrow!"

I'm not coming back tomorrow, Nazia wanted to shout, but instead she stood up and felt the woman's stare as she edged past her into the house.

"You people are all the same," Fatima muttered. "Always taking advantage and still expecting to get paid for wasting my time." She turned back to Shenaz. "I've been so busy telling your friend how to do things right that I haven't had a chance to make the bread. Go in the kitchen and finish making the roti. You may as well work to make up for her laziness."

For the next two hours Nazia worked harder than she ever had in her entire life. She scrubbed the bathrooms, dusted all the furniture, then hand washed three baskets of laundry and hung it out to dry on the lines behind the house. Her back ached in a strange way, and she felt as though ten-kilo bags of rice were strapped to her shoulders. Her clothes were soaked with sweat and dirty soap water.

As Nazia hung up the last of the laundry, all around her microphones came to life and charged the air with the call to prayer. As one mosque after another joined the *Azan*, the call to prayer became a rolling echo reverberating over the city.

Nazia's hands stilled and she lifted her eyes heavenward. *Please forgive me, Allah,* she prayed silently. Right now Maleeha and everyone else at the Gizri School for Girls would be rushing off to perform the ritual cleansing of *wazu* before standing up for *Zohar,* the afternoon prayer. She glanced down at her own clothes and wondered if Allah would even accept her wazu. Feeling too dirty and tired to pray, Nazia made the painstaking choice to forgo the mandatory prayer.

Maybe I could make it up when I'm finished, Nazia thought hopefully, and went back inside. She shook off her remorse and tried to distract herself as she moved through the house. While she cleaned, Nazia marveled at the teakwood furniture and ornate chandeliers. The dining table was enormous, with matching teakwood chairs, and she wondered what it would be like to live in that house, eating at that table, under the sparkling light of colored-glass raindrops. A cabinet held dishes made of delicate china, so different from the aluminum plates her family ate on, the ones with the bottoms so warped that they no longer rested flat.

Despite her exhaustion, Nazia finished up the last of the cleaning as quickly as possible. She took one final run through the house, satisfied that even a prince would have been impressed with her work. She stopped at the mogul-style mirror in the main entryway and untied her dupatta from her waist. As she wiped the sweat from her honey-colored face, Nazia noticed the deeper hollows of her cheekbones. She was still hungry and wondered if the memsahib would offer her a meal.

Just then Fatima stepped into the entryway and motioned her to the kitchen, where Shenaz and Amma waited.

"Your daughter is a hard worker," Fatima said to Amma, smiling. "She works harder than you." She filled a plastic bag with rice and lentils, then pulled out some stale bread from the hot pot and handed them to Amma.

"Take this. You can come back tomorrow, but only if you bring the girl. You can't do this job alone."

Amma started to protest, but Fatima held up her hand. "The pay will be eight hundred rupees a month for the two of you. Take it or leave it."

Alarmed, Nazia moved closer to Amma and nudged her. Eight hundred rupees! You couldn't even buy a decent dress from Zainab Market with that. Not for her jahez, anyway. Nazia pleaded with her eyes, but when Amma wouldn't even look her way, her calves began to shake. "No!" she blurted out. It was one thing for Amma to drag her out here for one day, but to make her quit school? Abbu would be furious with them both!

She tugged at her mother's shoulder, but Amma turned only long enough to give her a reprimanding glare. *Don't spoil this,* her eyes commanded.

Nazia loosed her grip and lowered her voice to barely a whisper so only Amma could hear. "Please, Amma! I can't fall behind.

Abbu would never allow me to miss school. Why are you trying to make things worse for us?"

Amma brushed Nazia away with an impatient hand and proceeded to negotiate with Fatima. Nazia stood behind her in silence as she willed her mother to say no and walk away, but it was no use.

Amma's protests were lame, and Shenaz was only halfhearted in her attempts to convince Fatima to raise the pay. In the end Amma accepted the deal. To make matters worse, an advance was out of the question, and there would be no payment until the month's end. When the deal was sealed, Nazia picked up Mateen and followed Amma and Shenaz to the gate. With her eyes downcast, and her body limp with exhaustion, Nazia reluctantly ignored Isha's plaintive cries to be carried too.

What had Shenaz gotten them into?

Later they sat in the shade of a *neem* tree and ate the meal straight out of the plastic bag. The break was painfully short, and they moved on to the next house, where Nazia again helped her mother clean, this time moving faster since their hunger was sated and the house was smaller. When they reached the third house, the sun had dipped farther toward the horizon and long shadows fell on the ground.

Black paint peeled from the sheet-metal gate, and there were cracks in the concrete driveway. Shenaz rang the buzzer, and a boy about Isha's age swung open the gate.

"Look who's here!" The boy pranced around on bare feet.

"You're late." He ushered them inside, bolted the gate, and then ran back toward the house, hollering, "Baji! Seema baji! The masis are here!"

With Mateen on her hip and Isha holding on to her dupatta, Nazia trudged behind her mother up to the house. The bougain-villea grew wildly over the low wall, the magenta-colored flow-ers withered and dry. Patches of dry earth were visible between the thatches of brown grass, and a large coconut tree offered the only shade.

The wrought-iron grilles that covered the windows were rusted a deep bronze. Nazia stood with Mateen asleep against her as she listened to the new memsahib go over their duties. The pay was two hundred less than the other two houses, but the work was much lighter. She breathed a sigh of relief when Seema said the house needed only sweeping and mopping since the day was almost done. Nazia laid Mateen on the grass in the shade of the palm tree and ordered Isha to keep an eye on him. Isha collapsed beside her brother and closed her eyes. A wave of pity flushed through Nazia at the sight of her sister's exhaustion, but she turned away before the tears could spring.

The boy who had opened the gate watched them, his head cocked to one side, his brows furrowed together. "She's not going to help?"

"Of course not." Nazia removed her dupatta from her shoulders and tied it tightly at her hip. "She's only ten years old."

"Ten." The boy's mouth twisted in a quizzical expression. "So I must be ten, right?"

Nazia looked at the boy. He was barely taller than Isha. His hair was jet black, but coarse from lack of washing. He wore a common kurta and pajama, pale blue, too big. His eyes were large, and he flashed a toothy grin and wiggled his eyebrows at her. "Don't you know your own age?" she asked.

He shrugged.

"I'd say you're ten. Is the memsahib — I mean Seema baji — your mother?"

The boy grabbed his belly, doubling over in hysterical laughter.

"Why is that so funny?" Nazia snapped.

"Baji is baji. My mother lives near the railway station. I live here with baji and help her take care of the house. I can't do everything — that's why she told Shenaz baji to bring your *amma*."

Nazia tried to imagine this reed-thin boy doing all the cleaning. "What do you do?"

"I open the gate, take out the trash, run to the market, tend to the garden, make tea, rub baji's feet. Whatever she wants, I can do it." He puffed out his chest and thumped it. "Sherzad can do anything."

"Sherzad, eh? I'm Nazia." She waved a hand behind her. "Mateen and Isha, my brother and sister. So, you live here?"

He pointed to a small room built into the wall by the gate. "See over there? That's mine. I guard the house from thieves and killers every night."

Nazia snorted. "You're so small; they'd probably mistake you for a mouse."

Sherzad giggled and punched the air with his fist. "A killer mouse! A weasel! Even the cobras can't catch me." He bounced around and pretended to throw punches at her.

"Nazia!" Shenaz's shrill voice erupted from behind the front window. The screen was gray with dust, and her face was barely visible. "Get in here and help your mother. Sherzad! Leave her alone. They didn't come here to entertain you."

Sherzad stuck out his tongue at the sooty window and mimicked Shenaz. He giggled again when she hollered at him. "Go on," he said, still smiling as he walked away. "I have to finish hanging the laundry."

In less than an hour Nazia and her mother finished up and headed home. The baji didn't offer any food, and Amma didn't ask. They were simply grateful that the memsahib only needed the floor cleaned.

When they got home, they found Abbu lying on the mattress watching television. He started to get up, then fell back against the cushions. "Where have you been?"

Isha went to her father and collapsed on his chest. "Amma took us with her. She cleaned houses all day long, and I had to take care of Mateen."

Nazia splashed water on her face. She listened to her parents, waiting for Abbu's fury. Cleaning houses was something only the poor did. It was work that only the transient people would agree to do, the ones who left their villages up north to find some semblance of prosperity in the big city. Cleaning houses was something you did when no one else would hire you. Abbu would never tolerate the shame of his family's lowering themselves to this. He would make sure she stayed in school.

But Abbu asked Amma in a mild voice, "How much are they paying you?"

Nazia's hand slowed as she wiped the water from her face with her sweaty dupatta. *It will come,* she thought. *Abbu's indignation will come and rescue me.*

Amma put a pot of water on the stove for tea. "Two houses are eight hundred rupees apiece, and one house is paying six hundred." She moved out of the kitchen — which was nothing more than a corner of the small house, with no wall to muffle the sounds of clattering pans and running water.

There was a moment of silence. "Two thousand, two hundred rupees?" Abbu said, shaking his head in disbelief. "That's what I made at the construction site."

Amma made a small sound when she bent to sit on the floor on the other side of the room, far from her husband. She leaned against the wall and squeezed her eyes shut for a moment as she massaged her knees. Slowly she opened them and stared vacantly at the TV screen.

Nazia stayed in the kitchen waiting for the water to boil. Why wasn't Abbu upset? Yes, it was a lot of money — well, not a whole lot, but still. It was from cleaning rich people's toilets! Mateen waddled up with his hands outstretched and wrapped himself around Nazia's legs, begging to be lifted. She smoothed his hair and clucked at him, trying to silence him so she could hear her father.

"Naseem, you know I'll find work when I get better." His voice was cheery. "Can you imagine? If only Bilal wasn't such a duffer. I bet he could make at least as much, and then we'd have almost five thousand rupees a month. Five thousand rupees."

"Don't say that about my son," Amma snapped. "You know he left to find work. Bilal is a boy with a *degree*. He'll find something and make me proud."

Nazia handed a stale piece of bread to Mateen. He grabbed the roti and wriggled away to sit on Abbu's stomach, bouncing gleefully. Isha moved aside to rest her head in the crook of Abbu's arm.

So that's it? Nazia thought. Bilal's disappearance weighed so heavily on Abbu's mind that he wasn't grasping what Amma was saying. Maybe he would realize the horror of it when he understood that Amma intended to pull her out of school.

She made the *chai* and offered the tray of cups to her father first. He slid Mateen off his stomach and nudged Isha away before taking the good teacup. He looked at Nazia.

"Beta, you helped your mother?"

Although she was bent over with the tray outstretched, Nazia ignored the dull pain in her back while her father's eyes held hers. He was finally asking the right questions! She nodded eagerly.

"Good girl. Cleaning houses is hard work. Amma cannot do it alone. She needs you."

Nazia blinked at her father. Didn't he realize what that meant?

But he seemed oblivious to her shock and went on stirring sugar into his chai. "Bilal should be the one coming home telling me he found work." He settled back against the pillow and shook his head. "Only God knows where that lazy boy could be."

She wondered where Bilal could have gone. He disappeared for days on end with his friends, but he'd never been gone this long before. She offered the tray to her mother, who refused to meet her gaze. Without a word Nazia handed Amma the cracked cup, then returned to the kitchen to make dinner.

She filled a pan of orange lentils with water and skimmed away the gritty foam with her fingers. After putting the lentils on the stove to boil, she put on another pot of water for the rice. As she waited for the second pot to boil, she sifted through the rice and picked out tiny stones, discarding them in the sink. Amma's voice carried over the drama on PTV, the national channel.

"Nazia will have to leave the school."

Nazia's hand stilled.

Her father clicked his tongue. "What about Isha and Mateen?"

"Isha can still take the bus to school, if Mateen stays home with you."

"How would I care for him? It hurts for me to move around."

Amma was silent. Nazia turned the faucet on and rinsed the rice.

Abbu shifted his weight on the foam mattress and groaned. "You'll have to take them with you. Isha can go to school later. Nazia will be getting married soon anyway, so it doesn't matter. Let her husband send her to school if he wants."

It doesn't matter? If her husband wants? The second pot began to boil, and Nazia let the grains of rice fall in. But they fell too quickly, and boiling water splattered onto her hand, scalding her. "Ouch!" She slammed the pan on the counter.

"What is wrong?" her father called out.

Tell him, she shouted to herself. *Tell him everything's all wrong!* Instead she turned on the faucet and held her hand under the running water. "Nothing, Abbu. Nothing's wrong."

How could she make a fuss about her own selfish needs when Abbu was so overwhelmed by other, more pressing problems? Like a leg that didn't work or a son who'd been missing for weeks? He needed her to be strong. That was what he was trying to tell her. And so she would be, whether she wanted to or not.

That was it, then. There would be no more discussion about school. She wondered what Maleeha and Saira would say when she didn't show up tomorrow or the next day or the weeks after that. Would they still come to play with her? Or would she always come home too tired to see them? Would they even want to be her friends when they found out she was a masi? A servant to the wealthy? She stuck out her tongue to lick away salty tears. Outside, the call to *namaz* sounded again. Would she ever stand in prayer with her class fellows? Would she ever hear the tales of Ms. Haroon and her adventurous travels around the country? Would she ever go back to school again?

Nazia was on her knees mopping the kitchen floor at the last house of the day. Her pace had improved as the days passed, and she was able to be home by late afternoon, leaving time for Amma to keep up with her sewing. It was already mid September, and Amma was still working hard to build up the jahez for her daughter's wedding.

Nazia wiped the concrete floor with a dirty rag, occasionally dipping it in a bucket of murky soap water.

Sherzad swung open the screen door. "Where's Seema baji?"

Nazia shrugged and kept working.

Sherzad rattled the door. "Could you just get her? I'm going to die if she doesn't feed me soon."

Nazia's own stomach growled at the thought of food. She'd learned quickly that the bajis gave food on their own whims and were rarely considerate enough to ask if they were ever hungry.

Just then Seema lumbered into the kitchen, her hair mussed and her eyes heavy, as though she'd just woken from a fitful nap. Sherzad immediately perked up. "Baji, I've finished weeding the *kayari*. Can I have lunch now?"

"Coming, coming," she grumbled. She pulled his steel plate from the cabinet and filled it with day-old roti and soupy green lentils. She held it out, but Sherzad shook his head.

"Baji, please. Do I look like a bird? Even a bird would eat this and still be hungry."

"Don't be insolent." She frowned and shoved the plate closer to Sherzad. "Take it."

He crossed his arms, locking his hands under his armpits. "I've been cooking in the sun since morning to clean your garden, and this is all I get?" He glanced at the stove and took a deep, exaggerated whiff. "There's *gosht salan* over there. The fragrance from the beef curry is too strong to ignore. Baji, please. All you gave me for breakfast was chai and roti. I'm a growing boy." He stood on tiptoes. "I need meat."

Nazia suppressed a smile and ran the wet rag over Sherzad's foot. He didn't move.

Baji set the plate on the center island and placed her hands on her bulky hips. Lentils sloshed onto the chipped marble top. "What do you take me for? Your private cook?" Suddenly she grabbed

Sherzad by the front of his shirt and cuffed him on the head. Sherzad brought his arms to his head. Stunned, Nazia shrank back against the cabinets, partly hidden from view by the center island.

At that moment the sahib entered the kitchen, his cane slipping on the wet floor. "What's going on here?"

Nazia stood up, yanking her dupatta from her waist and draping it over her hair. "Sahib, be careful. The floor is wet."

He stopped, taking in Sherzad's hunched stance. He glared at his wife. "Seema, what is the matter with you? Why must you always hit the servants for no reason at all?"

"Stay out of it, Rashid. The servants are my problem, not yours."

Seema grabbed a rag and wiped up the green spill on the marble. She picked up the plate and thrust it at Sherzad, motioning for him to go outside. Sherzad took the plate gingerly and tried to slink out, but Rashid stopped him.

"Did you want more food?" he asked Sherzad.

"Nahi, sahib." Sherzad shook his head. "Baji gave me plenty."

The sahib walked stiffly to the stove, his worn shoes squeaking on the damp floor. He lifted the lid on the pot. "Beef curry." He gave his wife a sideways look. "Would it kill you to share the good stuff with the servants every now and then?"

"I'm warning you, Rashid. Don't disgrace me in front of my servants. They'll never listen to me if I don't keep them in line."

"Right. Always trying to keep everyone in your line," Rashid said with a sigh. "Well, I guess you never learned that kindness creates more loyalty. Not even with your children. You do remember we have children, don't you?"

Seema's face turned a dangerous shade of red. "They didn't

leave because of me!" She looked at Sherzad and Nazia. "Give them all of it," she sputtered. "Our money grows on trees, doesn't it? You can pick more notes from the branches and give those away too while you're at it." A stream of insults spewed continuously as she huffed out of the kitchen and walked away.

Rashid rested his cane against the cabinet and picked up the serving spoon. "Bring me your plate."

Sherzad looked at Nazia, but she shrugged and motioned for him to go to the sahib. It was the first time Nazia had ever run into the sahib since they'd started working at his house. She watched him as he ladled the beef onto Sherzad's plate. Peppery hair, closely clipped, encircled the back of his balding head like a crescent moon. His trousers were belted high at the waist, and his white shirt was dusty and wet across the back. She wondered where he spent his day, dressed so finely yet still grimy and sweaty.

After Sherzad left the room, the sahib reached for his cane and turned to Nazia. "I have two business associates in the drawing room. I need three cups of chai right away. And send in some cold water. The streets are boiling out there."

With Seema sulking in her room and Amma sweeping the walkway outside, Nazia had no choice but to brew and serve the tea herself. She carried the mopping rag and bucket to the outdoor basin and washed her hands under the faucet, then hurried back inside. She wanted to go check on Sherzad to make sure he was okay, but there was no time.

She spent the next half hour serving drinks and biscuits to aging men in suits and dusty shoes. They talked loudly and laughed suddenly, never acknowledging her presence.

Just before leaving, the sahib stopped Nazia in the kitchen. "*Shukriya*, beta. You did a fine job." He filled a steel bowl with gosht salan and handed it to her. "Share this with your family."

Nazia flushed with pride at the unexpected kindness and gratefully took the beef stew. When the cleaning was finished, she sat with her family in a tight circle on the veranda. As they scooped the food out, Nazia told her mother how Seema had struck Sherzad.

Amma merely grunted between bites, her indifference infuriating Nazia.

"He's no bigger than Isha. How can she do that to him?"

"How can she not? He's her servant. He should have known by now not to complain about his food."

"But the sahib scolded baji. He gave Sherzad the gosht even when baji wouldn't."

"Don't for one minute think that the sahib wouldn't have lifted a hand at the boy. Make no mistake about that. And just because you call the memsahib 'baji' doesn't make her care about you like a big sister would. Sahibs, memsahibs . . . they are all the same. We are nothing more than servants to them and never will be. Now be quiet and finish up."

"Well, I'm going to see if Sherzad is okay. Baji hit him pretty hard." Nazia began to stand, but Amma grabbed her wrist and pulled her back to the ground. Isha stopped eating and stared at her mother.

"Sit down and eat," Amma said crossly.

"But—"

"If you don't eat it, then feed it to Mateen or Isha." Her eyes softened. "It's gosht, beta. How often do we get meat, child?"

Nazia tore off a small piece of roti. Mateen was already at her side, and she shoved the morsel into his open mouth. She fed half the gosht to Mateen and ate the rest herself. When they were done, she rinsed the plates outside and set them on the ledge to dry while Amma told the memsahib that they were leaving for the day, then headed for the gate.

"Carry me," Mateen complained.

"You have feet," Nazia snapped. "Walk."

Isha looked crossly at Nazia before taking her brother's hand in hers, leading him to the gate. Nazia snatched their belongings and stomped after her mother. She didn't know if she was irritated at her mother for not caring more about Sherzad, or if she was mad at herself for eating the meat and enjoying every bite. Passing Sherzad's room, she could hear him sniffling inside. She edged closer to the door, but Amma stopped her.

"Stay out of it, Nazia. It's not your business."

"How can you walk past him, Amma, and not do anything? He's just a kid."

"He got what he wanted, didn't he? More food? Meat?"

Nazia couldn't understand why her mother was being so callous. She was always so tender with Mateen and Isha. "But baji hit him. Hard. What if he was Isha? Or Mateen?"

"But he's not, is he?" Amma asked, her voice tired. She draped her dupatta over her head, tucking the edges behind her ears to keep it from blowing off. "Let his own mother worry about him, beta. I have enough on my mind worrying about Bilal and what could be happening to him." Amma gave the gate a hard push and walked through without looking back.

When they returned home late in the after-
noon, the door was open and Abbu was nowhere in sight. Puzzled,
Nazia stepped inside. Before she could stop her, Amma pushed
past her, out of the blazing rays of the sun.

The house was in shambles. Nazia's heart hammered in her
ears as she looked at the mess, and Amma began to wail.

"Ya Allah! Ya Allah!"

The mattress was overturned and the pillows stripped of their
covers. Clothes and sheets were scattered across the floor, and
every cupboard in the kitchen was open, the contents strewn
across the counter, toppled over, and some on the floor. Amma
staggered to the small closet in the corner of the house, and Nazia
hurried after her when she realized what Amma was doing. When
Nazia reached down to help pull the heavy suitcase out of the
closet, she nearly fell backward as it sailed out of the closet,
weightless.

Amma whimpered as she yanked at the zipper of the oversized
bag. Nazia watched her mother fumble with the metal teeth. Who
would bother to zip up a suitcase after stealing everything inside
it? Still, when Amma flung the lid open, the emptiness hit her

with unexpected force. Amma collapsed over the empty bag, her body heaving as she sobbed. Nazia laid a hand over her mother's shaking back. All of her dowry was gone. The gold bangles, the necklaces, the earrings, a lifetime's worth of savings. Even the intricately beaded garments, designed to be worn only after her wedding, were missing.

Mateen jumped into the suitcase and pressed himself against his mother and began crying too. Nazia motioned to Isha to help calm the boy. Isha remained by the door, her eyes wide with fear as she shook her head and refused to move.

"Amma." Nazia wanted to say, *Don't worry; it was only clothes and jewelry.* But they both knew it was more than that. Nazia held Mateen on her lap while he cried. Vivid memories flashed through her mind as she recalled the times her mother had come home with velvet boxes filled with gold and precious stones. Every year Amma added a necklace or a pair of earrings to the dowry. Small but precious offerings for a daughter's security.

Nazia tried to soothe Amma's pain, but it was no use. Years of hard work were wiped out in a single blow, and she realized that it would take Amma a long time to recover. She tended to her siblings, comforting them with a few soft words, then began the arduous task of cleaning. As she picked up the debris and replaced the sheets, she couldn't help wondering where her father had gone. He should have been here. This never would have happened if he had been home. When Amma's moans subsided to sniffles, Nazia pulled her mother to her feet and helped her to the bed. Amma crumpled onto the mattress and buried her face in the pillow.

Even though the stolen jewelry was hers, Nazia felt no attachment to it, at least not in the way Amma did. Amma was the one who had skimmed money Abbu had given her for food and clothes, tucking it away year after year. The thief had robbed Amma, not her.

But as Nazia smoothed her mother's hair, a new thought crept into her head. After only a few weeks of cleaning houses Nazia had begun wondering if life would be easier when she married her cousin and moved back to their village. It was a daydream that made the cleaning jobs go by faster. But with no dowry, there was a real possibility that the wedding would be postponed. No girl she'd ever known had gotten married without a dowry.

Nazia turned on the TV for her brother and sister, then sat outside to wait for Abbu. Within minutes Maleeha came out of her house and rushed over.

"Did he take everything?" Maleeha asked, her voice cautious.

Nazia stared at her. "How did you know we were robbed?"

"Just *tell* me, what did he take?"

"The only thing taken was the jewelry and some of the clothes for my dowry. It was all in a suitcase." She peered at Maleeha. "Why would they take my clothes?"

"It wasn't a they," Maleeha said fervently. "It was a *him*. And he's probably going to sell them to a shopkeeper."

Nazia gaped at her friend in sudden realization. "You saw him? You know who did this?"

Maleeha nodded. "I came over thinking you were home. I knocked on the door because I could hear noises from inside, but the door was already open. So I gave it a little push and called you. Only you weren't there." Maleeha grabbed her hand and squeezed. "But your brother Bilal was."

Nazia curled her fingers around Maleeha's hand, not trusting herself to speak.

"I saw him with my own eyes." Maleeha peeked inside the doorway before speaking again, her voice hushed. "He tore everything apart. Like he was looking for something. I guess he knew your mother must have kept the jewelry in the house. He had everything in a shoulder bag, like a backpack, and he left on his motorcycle."

Nazia pulled her hands away and hugged herself. When she finally spoke, her voice shook. "Did you see Abbu?"

"No." Maleeha's brows knitted together. "Are you going to be okay?"

Nazia sighed. "Just don't tell Amma it was Bilal. The news will kill her."

"I won't. Are you sure you don't need anything? I can ask my mother to send some food, if you want. I didn't tell her about seeing Bilal, though." Maleeha rolled her eyes. "You know how she is. The whole neighborhood will know by nightfall if she finds out."

"No. It'll get back to Amma somehow if you tell her." Nazia stood and shook the dust from her shalwar. "I'll see if there are any leftovers. If not, I'll cook some rice or something." She gave Maleeha a fierce hug. "Thank you."

Maleeha's smile faltered. "I guess this means you really aren't coming back to school anytime soon, huh? Ms. Haroon keeps asking about you."

Nazia was surprised at how quickly the tears sprang up.

"Oh, I'm sorry." Maleeha grabbed her dupatta and wiped Nazia's face before she could back away. "I didn't mean to do that, it's just that I . . . we miss you, that's all."

Nazia nodded. "It's okay. I'm fine." She sucked in a deep breath and exhaled loudly. "I'll do whatever I must to help Amma. I just don't understand why he would steal from us. He must know that Amma misses him." She looked off into the distance, at the diehard cricket players indifferent to the relentless heat.

Maleeha shook her head. "I don't know. He didn't look good, though — he seemed thinner and meaner, I guess. I should know, remember? I always thought he was cute." A startled look crossed her face. "But he doesn't know I saw him, and I'm pretty sure he didn't see me, so if he comes back, don't tell him I ratted on him."

"I won't."

After Maleeha left, Nazia stood for a few more minutes watching the cricketers play. Why couldn't her brother have been like one of them? Even if these boys were considered lazy for spending every minute after school playing cricket, at least their mothers could stand outside their doorways and holler for them to come home. At least they were there when their families needed them. Now she knew for certain that Bilal would never come to their rescue the way Amma believed.

Even though Amma deserved to know the truth, Nazia vowed that she wouldn't be the one to shatter her faith. She would carry the secret of his betrayal for as long as she could, until the weight of the knowledge dragged her down and she could no longer climb up the hill to clean houses with Amma.

———— ►◄ ————

At Fatima's house the next morning Nazia swept the veranda in slow arcs. She was lost in thought, still shocked by Bilal's betrayal, and didn't notice Fatima baji watching her curiously from inside. The creak of the screen door barely registered in her brain, and it wasn't until the memsahib shook her arm that she broke out of her reverie.

"What's wrong, beta?" Fatima asked.

Nazia looked up at her, then away when she saw that her concern was genuine. "Nothing," she mumbled.

"There must be something. You and your mother look so sad, and the younger ones aren't here today. Are they sick?"

"No. Abbu kept them with him today."

Fatima crossed her arms, waiting. "You don't have to tell me if you don't want to."

The screen door creaked and Amma joined them on the veranda. "We were robbed last night, baji. Nazia's jahez is gone."

Fatima clucked her tongue. "They took her dowry?"

Amma nodded.

"But wasn't your husband home? I thought he broke his leg?"

"Nahi." Amma snorted. "He's fine. He's just decided that he doesn't need to work. All our men are like that, you know. I thought he would be different. It just took him longer, that's all."

Nazia stopped sweeping. How could Amma speak so harshly about Abbu? Maybe he wasn't looking for work as quickly as he should be, but that was no reason to be disloyal to him.

"Well, do you think he stole it?" Fatima asked.

Nazia dropped the broom. "Of course not! You don't even know him!"

"Now, Nazia, I thought he might have." Amma sat down on the veranda steps, wiping sweat off her face with the bottom of her kameeze. "When he came home last night, he seemed just as upset as me, so I can't be sure. I don't know. I'm too tired to speculate."

"Well, I can't offer you much else but to pay you early, so here it is." Fatima reached inside her kameeze and pulled out the folded rupees. She started to walk back into the house, then stopped. "I have some extra things you can take with you when you leave today. Vegetables with rice. Some biscuits for the children. I'll pack it up for you."

Amma only nodded.

So there it was. Fatima's hidden good side. Nazia knew she should be grateful for baji's kindness, but she couldn't help feeling shamed by the pity she saw in the woman's eyes. And the betrayal she'd just heard from her mother's lips.

She watched her mother and tried to understand what she was going through. Which was worse for Amma? Believing your husband robbed you or knowing it was your son? Amma already believed that Abbu was faking the seriousness of his injuries and intentionally dragging out his recovery. But did she really think so little of him that she could believe so quickly that he was the one who stole her jahez?

Nazia picked up the broom to continue sweeping the veranda, her brow furrowed as she wondered how Amma could believe Abbu to be so heartless. He was always there to care for them even when her brother wasn't. She would keep silent about Bilal, but she needed her mother to be more faithful.

Nazia stopped sweeping and sat down beside her mother. She pressed her hands to Amma's knees and forced her to look at her. "Abbu didn't take my jahez. I know it."

Amma sighed. "You are practically a woman, and yet you still see everything through the eyes of a child."

Nazia shook her mother's knees in frustration. "I'm not blind, Amma, but I know he didn't take it. I cannot tell you how I know, but I know it."

"I worry about your thoughts, beta." Amma cupped Nazia's face with both hands. "They are clouded, willful, and not suited for a girl so close to marriage. I am awake late into the night because I worry for you."

"Amma, you should sleep instead," Nazia replied lightly. "Then maybe you wouldn't be so tired."

"Who knows when Allah plans to grant you wisdom? For your sake I pray it is soon."

Amma dropped her hands and closed her eyes. Nazia stared at her mother's sparse eyelashes and realized that she had to convince Abbu that he needed to go back to work. It was the only way Amma would believe in him again.

Amma kept some of the money and gave the rest to Abbu when they went home that evening. "Now, don't you stop anywhere," she warned. "Take that straight to Iqbal for the rent, and tell him from now on we won't fall behind."

"Mateen and Isha have been making me crazy the whole day. I need to get some air. Don't worry. I'll pay Iqbal sahib and be home by the last prayer." Abbu stuffed the money into his kurta pocket and slipped on his worn leather sandals before heading out the door. "Go ahead and eat dinner without me," he called behind him. "I'll grab something along the way."

Amma moved quickly to the doorway. "You'd better not spend the rent on your fat belly!" She turned back and muttered, "I should have taken the money to Iqbal myself."

Abbu had insisted on taking the rent to the landlord, admitting he was well enough to take the bus. Nazia hoped that his admission of health meant that his spirits were improving. Once the rent was paid, it would be one less thing for her parents to worry about. Tomorrow she would nudge him about finding work. Maybe even offer to walk with him to Gizri and share a cold glass of yogurt *lassi.*

"He'll take care of it," Nazia said. "I guess he's trying, isn't he?" She wasn't so sure anymore, but there was no point in letting Amma know her doubts. "He watched Isha and Mateen all day, and he even told us he was feeling better. He'll find a job soon, Amma. Just be patient."

"Hmph," Amma snorted. "He's just sitting around to see how much we will do when he does nothing."

"Well, I don't believe that," Nazia said firmly. "Abbu has always taken care of us, and there's no reason for him to stop now." She looked into her mother's amber-colored eyes. "And just forget about what baji said. Abbu would never steal my dowry or destroy our house. Someone else did it, so just forget about it."

Nazia could almost hear her mother tallying up the years that had gone into putting the dowry together. No one in their neighborhood would risk putting such precious valuables in a bank for safekeeping, but then no one would ever have expected their own son to steal from them.

"Cheer up." She waved the sack of food Fatima had given them. "We don't have to cook dinner tonight. But first we'll have a nice cup of tea and some biscuits."

Amma caressed Nazia's cheek, her tone suddenly somber. "You are the light of my life, beta. You know that, don't you?"

Nazia smiled. "I know, Amma."

"Whatever I do, it is only to ensure your happiness, your future."

"Amma, please, I know all that."

"It pains me to have you clean with me, but I have no choice. You see that, don't you?" Amma pulled her daughter close. "I see how hard you work. You are my strength, beta. With the jahez gone, I need your help for just a little longer."

"I'll always do whatever you want, Amma. You know that." Nazia pressed her face in the crook of Amma's neck, breathing in the scent of jasmine, tangy sweat, and mustard oil.

Amma pulled away and looked at Nazia worriedly. "Sometimes I wonder. You are the perfect daughter, but your will is strong. Sometimes, I think, stronger than mine."

"Amma, stop worrying. You know I will always do whatever must be done."

"That is what I love about you, beta. But that is also what I'm afraid of."

Nazia wiped away the tear that slipped from the corner of Amma's eye. She knew that her mother was just upset about the lost dowry, but why did she get the strange feeling that there was something else? That Amma was trying to warn her about something? She shook off the feeling and gave her mother a hug. There was money for rent and they had food for the night. *For once let there be joy,* she thought. "Go sit down, Amma, and stop your worrying. I'll make the tea."

Nazia prepared the tea while her mother went outside, where a neighbor hovered near their doorway, eager to chat. Nazia poured an extra cup and set it on a tray with half of the biscuits.

She carried the tray outside and distributed the tea and biscuits. She grinned at Mateen and Isha as she watched them devour the first biscuit, then nibble slowly on the next one, savoring every crumb. Nazia took her cup and settled in beside them to watch the field teeming with kids, the murmur of her mother and neighbor chatting behind them. Older boys had taken over the cricket pitch, and a serious competition was in progress. Nazia spotted Maleeha and Saira on the edge of the pitch, feigning boredom. Nazia squinted. Was Maleeha wearing that pink material from the cloth market? It was far too fancy for ordinary use, and Nazia wondered if Maleeha's mother had just sewn it for her and she was showing off in front of the cricketers.

She dipped her cumin biscuit into the tea and let the shortbread melt on her tongue. She never used to drink tea, but ever since she'd started working, Nazia found that tea contained some miracle concoction that soothed away her aches and calmed her nerves.

She touched a corner of her shirt, the colors faded, the cotton thinning. She wondered whether, if she went and stood with Saira and Maleeha, any of the cricket players would notice her. Her hair had turned coppery under the daily glare of the sweltering sun, and her skin had browned, with freckles popping up everywhere. Blue veins strained against the backs of her hands, and her feet had grown flatter with tough calluses from rubbing against the concrete and marble floors as she worked barefoot throughout the houses. But what bothered her the most were the dark circles under her eyes. They were like half-moons dented into her skin, a bluish hue that cast a shadow over her cheeks, just like Amma's.

Would her cousin Salman think her even passably pretty? Would he still insist on marrying her, or would he cringe when he laid eyes on her? They needed to start rebuilding the dowry, for Amma's sake. Nazia knew that her mother would not be able to rest until there was enough to ensure her daughter's marriage. How long would that take? How could years of savings be replaced in just a few short months? Abbu *had* to find work. He just had to!

It was almost midnight when Abbu slipped into the house. The lights were off, but the glow of the television was enough for Nazia to see by his limp shoulders that they were about to be visited by more bad news. She remained lying on the floor, squeezed next to Isha and Mateen, and waited for him to speak. Amma was on him like ants on cake, asking if he'd paid the rent.

He held up a hand to silence her. "The money is gone."

Amma moaned as she flung herself upon her husband and thrashed him with her fists, landing punches wherever she could. Nazia stood and tried to stop her, but Abbu had already pushed Amma back against the bulky cushions on the floor.

"Listen to me!" Abbu growled, pulling on the cord of the hanging bulb. Nazia blinked rapidly at the naked light.

"I was on my way to Iqbal's house after I ate."

"Lies!" Amma wailed, and lunged at him again.

Nazia yelled at her mother to stop, but Abbu already had his hands clamped over Amma's wrists.

"I was attacked by two men on a motorbike. They had a gun and took everything I had. I didn't even have bus fare to get home."

Amma continued to curse and kick at him with her stumpy legs until he released her. Nazia stared at him for a moment before returning to Isha and Mateen, who scooted closer as soon as she lay down. Her parents continued to scream at each other.

"What's going to happen now?" Isha whispered, her voice quivering.

Nazia rubbed her sister's stomach. "Go to sleep. We'll figure it out in the morning." She knew that the voices carried down the street, and by midday everyone would know that Abbu had lost the rent. When Amma accused Abbu of stealing the dowry, the sudden sound of a hand against flesh reverberated within her, leaving her immobile. She wanted to jump up and shout, *Stop! It was Bilal who took it — not Abbu!* But she was too afraid to move. Nazia feigned sleep when Abbu came close to the bed and pulled the light switch. She welcomed the darkness as it hid her tears that slid easily onto the packed-cotton pillow.

——————◄——————

The next day Nazia stood in Seema's kitchen washing the lunch dishes. She rubbed the yellow cake of soap with the rag to build up lather and wiped the cloth over the glasses and plates. Seema baji had made beef and potato stew and sent Sherzad out earlier for the *naan* from the bazaar. The bowl of leftovers sat uncovered on the center table, and Nazia eyed it longingly. Today's lunch had been stale bread and lentils that had gone bad. Amma had taken one whiff and thrown it in the dirt.

Seema baji had given them lunch before Amma and Nazia had started the cleaning, since they'd arrived much later than usual. Earlier that morning Nazia had stayed home to watch her siblings while Amma took the bus with Abbu to Tariq Road to speak to the landlord, but Iqbal would hear none of it. There were plenty of people willing to take their place in the cramped quarters where they lived, and Amma and Abbu's pleading made no difference. Amma had said that when Abbu told the story about being robbed last night, Iqbal threw his head back and laughed. It was the same story he heard every week from other renters who squandered their money. The landlord said they had until tomorrow night to get out.

Nazia pushed away her thoughts when Sherzad entered the kitchen. He set his empty plate on the table, and before she could stop him, he stuck his fingers into the stew and popped a piece of beef into his mouth. He pressed a finger to his lips as he gulped down the food. He ran to the door of the kitchen and peeked into the lounge.

"Baji is taking a nap," Nazia whispered.

Sherzad scooped another spoonful of stew onto his plate and grabbed a piece of naan from the counter.

She stopped washing. "You want another beating?"

He shrugged and took the plate of food outside. He was such a small thing for a ten-year-old. She'd seen the way he put all his energy into whatever he was doing, whether it was sweeping the driveway or cleaning the yard or doing the laundry. She couldn't imagine Isha having to take on such work and still be starving. Nazia poured a glass of water into the stew and stirred the mixture so the bowl still looked full. At least one of them wouldn't go hungry today.

Amma came in as Nazia was drying her hands on her dupatta. "Where's baji?"

"She's sleeping."

"Are you finished here?"

Nazia nodded.

"Let's go back to Fatima's house. Maybe she can offer us a place to stay. Abbu is looking, but I don't think he'll have any luck. If she says no, then we'll come back and ask Seema baji tomorrow."

"What about the memsahib from the second house? Her house is not far from Seema's place."

"I've already thought of that. We only clean the bathrooms and sweep the floor there. I don't think the memsahib at that house will make room for us, since we do so little for her. Besides, her quarters are already taken by her live-in servants."

Nazia pulled the edge of her dupatta over her head and stepped outside into her slippers. Mateen and Isha had fallen asleep under the shade of the veranda, and reluctantly she shook them. "Wake up. We're leaving."

Mateen whined to be carried and she obliged, pulling Isha along by the hand as they followed Amma to the gate and back onto the dusty road. The sun was hazy, and Nazia's feet burned inside the slippers. She passed Sherzad's quarters and stopped when he called out to her.

"You won't tell, will you?" He sat on his charpai, his empty plate beside him.

She shook her head. "Can't you go to the market and buy a kebab roll or something?"

He spread out his hands. "No money."

"What happens to your money?"

"Amma comes and takes it. She leaves me some, but I usually spend it on the first day." He cocked his head. "She doesn't leave me much, only ten or twenty rupees."

"That's it for the whole month?" Nazia asked in surprise.

"Well, Amma knows that baji is supposed to give me food and clothes, but it's not enough. Sometimes—"

"Hurry up, Nazia," Amma interrupted. "We don't have all day."

"Gotta go." She looked at Sherzad apologetically. "If I had the money, I'd give it to you. Maybe tomorrow I can bring you left-overs. I'll see what I can do." Nazia waved and caught up with her mother, but with Mateen in her arms and Isha hanging on to her kameeze, she struggled.

"Amma, slow down!"

Her mother didn't slow, and by the time they reached Fatima's house, Nazia was panting. She put Mateen down and bent over to catch her breath while they waited for the gate to open.

Amma laughed nervously when Fatima herself opened it. "Baji, what happened to your *chowkidar?*"

Fatima sighed. "He left this afternoon to help harvest the fields back home. He always does that at this time of year, but there is never anyone to take his place. My guard left too, to visit his family, but they both promised to come back in a few weeks. We'll see. What are you doing here? Did you forget something?"

"Nahi, nahi," Amma said. "Can we come in?"

Fatima's eyes narrowed slightly before she answered. "Is everything okay? Did you find out who robbed you?" She widened the gate for them.

"Nahi, baji. How will we ever find out? It's gone — that's all that matters now."

Fatima motioned for them to sit on the lawn, while she perched herself on the ledge that boxed in the jasmine shrubs. "So, tell me. What's going on?"

Nazia played with a blade of grass as she listened to her mother explain how Abbu had lost the money Fatima had given them, about the landlord evicting them, and their need for a place to stay. Fatima looked at Nazia, but Nazia averted her eyes, ashamed that Amma's voice sounded too much like begging.

"Well," Fatima said finally. "As I told you before, my chowkidar and guard will be back, and they have families as well who stay in the servant quarters. I don't have the space for your family, Naseem, but I can probably make room for one of you. If you want to leave Nazia with me, I'd make sure she was well taken care of."

Nazia lifted her head. Only her? The possibility of living apart from the family had never occurred to her. She could not recall spending a single night away from her mother, away from her own home.

"Nahi, baji——" Amma shook her head.

"She could stay inside the house, if you are worried about her safety. I could clean one of the servant rooms out back that's used for storage now, and she could keep her things there and use it in the day, but at night she could sleep in the reception area or the dining room, where she'd be safer."

Nazia twisted the grass around her fingers and snuck a glance at Fatima. What would it be like to live in the house with the iced teardrops over the dining table and Persian rugs to sleep on? Here would she be able to let go of her family's burdens and be content as baji's house servant? Could she really live without her family?

Nazia knew she was not street smart like Shenaz or book smart like Ms. Haroon. Or brave like Sherzad. It was an impossible proposition. One that she knew Amma would never agree to.

"Baji." Amma stood up. "Thank you, baji, for your kindness, but I can't leave my daughter alone. You know that. You know how the men are and how the other servants will talk. She's going to be married soon, and I won't put her innocence in jeopardy."

Fatima touched Nazia's head with the palms of her hands. "Naseem, your daughter will be safe here. I know I have a son, but he is away. The other men here would not dare bother Nazia so long as I'm here."

"Nahi. We will find something, baji. Don't worry. Allah will watch out for us when the time comes. He won't put us to live on the streets."

Nazia's eyes smarted. She wished fleetingly that she could stay with Fatima. Discreetly she lifted the corner of her dupatta and wiped her eyes. The sense of loss over something that she knew nothing about was strangely overwhelming. Was this one of those willful thoughts that Amma worried about?

Fatima sighed. "I'm sorry, Naseem. I wish I could help you more, but my servants will be back soon or you know I would take your whole family, don't you? They've been with me for three years now, and in today's climate that's a loyalty hard to find."

Amma took Isha's hand and stepped onto the driveway. When she slid her slippers on, Nazia stood too, taking Mateen with her. The sympathy in Fatima's eyes was undeniable. But Nazia couldn't help but think of the beatings Sherzad suffered when his mother wasn't there. Would this baji too suddenly become a different person when Amma left?

Amma had said all bajis were the same. Nazia didn't want to believe it, and she couldn't imagine that Fatima would do anything more than scold her. But it didn't matter anymore. Amma had refused, and now they would ask Seema tomorrow. Nazia glanced back at Fatima as she said good-bye at the gate, and at the unknown possibilities that slipped away.

After dinner Amma wandered about the sparsely furnished house, sifting through their clothes, sheets, and cookware. She lifted a round plastic clock from the wall and tossed it into the open suitcase that used to hold Nazia's jahez. Although it pained her to watch Amma pack away their meager possessions, Nazia knew she was only preparing for the inevitable. If they didn't find a place soon, by this time tomorrow they would be out on the street.

The night air was heavy with damp heat and the accumulated fumes from nearby traffic. Nazia sat in the open doorway in the hopes of catching a breeze, but nothing stirred. She spotted the lanky shape of a man striding toward her in the distance. She squinted, then relaxed when she realized it wasn't Abbu.

When he didn't veer off toward one of the other houses, she craned her neck as she watched him come toward her. Who could he be?

A gravelly voice called out. "Nazia? Is that you?"

Nazia stood quickly and draped her dupatta on her head just as the man reached her, his thin frame towering over her.

He touched her head lightly. "Nazia, beta. Don't you recognize me?"

Nazia peered up into his face. His eyes were hidden behind a large pair of thick-rimmed glasses, and a thin graying mustache lined his upper lip. Uncle Tariq!

"As salam-o-alaikum," she said slowly.

What was he doing here? Had Abbu contacted him about the missing dowry? She backed away to go into the house.

"Abbu isn't home, but Amma is. Please come in." She wanted to warn her mother, but Uncle Tariq was right behind her, his greeting a booming invasion in the small house.

Amma hurriedly dropped a cloth into the suitcase and smiled broadly. "Tariq bhai! What a pleasant surprise."

At Nazia's gentle prodding Isha moved Mateen from the small sofa and settled him on the mattress to make room for Uncle Tariq. The man sank into the cushions with his knees jutting awkwardly close to his chest. He rested his wide hands on his thighs and looked around the disheveled room. Nazia sidled over to the suitcase, flipping over the lid to cover their belongings.

"Where is Saleem?"

"I'm not sure." Amma's voice cracked when she spoke. "But he'll be home soon, and I know he'll be happy to see you. You must be hungry after your long train ride. Did you come straight from the station? You should have told us you were coming, and then I could have prepared a proper meal."

"Would you have had the time?" The knob in Uncle Tariq's throat bobbed up and down. "Naseem, you probably don't even have the strength to cook for your own family."

Amma clasped her hands behind her back. "What do you mean? Of course I can cook."

Uncle Tariq pushed his glasses up on his bony nose and gave Amma a worried look. "I mean with the houses you clean all over Karachi. You must be exhausted."

Amma blinked rapidly. "Tariq bhai, please let me explain. There is so much you do not know."

"I know more than you think, I'm afraid. One of the villagers who worked at the site where Saleem was injured came home a few days ago and brought me the news of his accident. Naturally, I was worried about my brother." He removed his glasses and began wiping the lenses with a corner of his kurta. "I do not understand how my brother can break his legs."

"His injuries were not that severe, and he is getting better——"

Uncle Tariq shook his head. "But he was injured enough to lose his job, right? Why didn't he inform me? How long has it been? Almost two months?"

Nazia stepped forward. "Uncle Tariq, we didn't want to worry you."

He put his glasses back on. "Not worry me? Beta, I have been half out of my mind with worry. Your abbu is the only brother I have. He is precious to me, and most importantly, his daughter is precious to me."

Nazia's cheeks reddened.

"I came because I have heard nothing from Saleem, and the villager's news about his injuries was concerning to me as well as my son. Salman asked me to come to Karachi to check on his future wife, to find out if your family needed anything. I thought maybe Saleem could use my help after the accident, some money for food or rent until his injuries healed." He shook his head. "I came in on the early-morning train today."

Uncle Tariq struggled to pull himself up from the sofa, his shoulders hunched and his brows drawn together. He clasped his wrists behind his back and began pacing in the cramped space.

"When I came this morning, no one was here, not even Saleem. I went to the neighbors, and they told me stories that I could not bring myself to believe. They said that Saleem is a worthless loafer, his son is missing, and his wife and daughter are working as masis! Naseem, is this true? Masis?"

Nazia wished that she could say something to ease her uncle's shock. Clearly the news of them working as masis was more upsetting than Abbu's injuries. Suddenly she realized that Amma might have been wrong about not asking for money from Uncle Tariq in the first place. Perhaps he would have gladly given them the money rather than see his soon-to-be daughter-in-law become a masi. But would he have thought less of her? She clenched her fists and prayed Amma could soothe him.

Amma wiped her dupatta over her face. "Saleem's recovery has taken some time, but he'll soon be working again. Tariq bhai, Nazia and I work only to pay for what we need. The rent. Our food. The money must come from somewhere."

"But as a masi, Naseem? How could you make such a decision for Nazia without coming to me first? I trusted you and Saleem to take care of her while you were in Karachi. She is your daughter for only a short time, but she will be my son's wife for the rest of her life."

Nazia cringed. He was embarrassed by her!

Amma's expression turned grim. "You think I enjoy cleaning houses? Or doing the bidding of the memsahibs until my back is near breaking? Do you think I would do anything to endanger my daughter? We do what has to be done. Now, let me make you some tea, and then I will start on the food."

"Sit down, sit down," he said, exasperated.

Nazia braced herself as Uncle Tariq grabbed her hands and examined her palms. "See this? I knew it. Look at these masi's hands." He clucked his tongue. "Look at the poor girl. Her hands are hard and callused like a man's." He stared at Nazia and dropped his voice. "If your father was ill and your mother was making you clean houses, you at least could have sent word to me. I would have helped you, beta."

Nazia squirmed under her uncle's gaze. Would he have been able to keep her in school? she wondered. Would he still feel the same when he learned the jahez was gone?

He turned back to Amma. "Is this the girl whom Saleem promised to my son? You are exposing your daughter to the world for what? Some money? You all should have come to me after the accident. Saleem swore to me that he would take care of you all in Karachi, especially Nazia, and had I known he'd go back on his word, I'd never have let him bring you here in the first place. Not when Nazia is already spoken for."

"I know she is spoken for. I didn't tell you because of her wedding. I wanted to be sure we had enough to pay for the wedding."

Uncle Tariq sat down again, his voice tired. "You think I care more about the price of the wedding than the quality of the bride? Look at her, Naseem. How can I let my son marry a masi? What will everyone back home say? I just don't understand why Saleem never sent word to the village."

"I'll tell you why." Amma crossed her arms. "Bilal disappeared before the accident. I know he left to find work, because he took some of his clothes and his motorbike. On top of that, Nazia's jahez was stolen."

"What?"

"That's right. Saleem was still sick, and there was no way to pay the rent. I was afraid that when you learned the jahez was gone, you would postpone the wedding."

Now he knew about the missing dowry. Would he delay the wedding? Nazia was confused by her own conflicting thoughts. Did she want the wedding postponed? If the marriage was delayed, would she have to continue working? If she married Salman, would she be able to finish school? Nazia felt the weight of her uncle's troubled gaze, and she averted her eyes in case he could read her mind.

Uncle Tariq cracked his knuckles. "Well, of course the dowry is critical in marriages, in every marriage. Just because Saleem and I are brothers makes no difference in the matter of the dowry."

"And knowing that, how could we have come to you for help?" Amma's eyes narrowed. "That is why we kept on working. To rebuild the jahez so my Nazia could come into your house and hold her head high. But what's the point? All our hard work was for nothing."

"What do you mean 'for nothing'?" He turned to Nazia. "What does she mean?"

Nazia moved closer to the sofa. "Amma gave Abbu the money we earned to pay the landlord for rent. But he was robbed on the way. When we tried to explain, the landlord wouldn't give us any more time. We must leave this house by tomorrow."

"Maybe we can go back to the village with you." Amma touched Uncle Tariq's sleeve. "Saleem can rest there, and Nazia will be herself again. The air will soften her skin, and her sun spots will fade. When he is well, Saleem can return to Karachi alone. He'll send money home; then the marriage can go on as planned."

Nazia remained silent. Her fate rested with her uncle, and there was no way around it.

He swallowed nervously. "I don't know."

"Please, Tariq bhai." Amma retracted her hand. "At least wait for your brother and talk to him yourself."

He looked at Nazia and Amma, then behind them at the children sitting on the mattress. "All right," he said finally. "I'll stay here tonight. When Saleem comes home, then we'll decide what's best for our families. Don't worry yourself. Now, all this talking has made me hungry."

Amma forced a smile and moved toward the kitchen. "We can fix that," she said. "By the time I'm finished cooking, Saleem should be home, and you can eat the meal together. Nazia, hurry and get the rice started."

Nazia followed her mother, and they set about preparing the meal. She prayed Abbu would return soon and appease his worried brother. She heard the television snap to life, blaring loudly in the background as Uncle Tariq made himself at home.

The following day Nazia stood in front of Maleeha's house, her best friend's arms clamped around her as they watched the landlord escort the new tenants into her home. Nazia twisted her dupatta around her fists and pressed them against her mouth, trying hard to keep the swell of rage from choking her. Her face burned as she recalled the way her mother had wrapped herself around Uncle Tariq's legs only a few hours ago, all the while insisting that Abbu would be home soon.

Uncle Tariq had waited until nearly four in the afternoon, but Abbu never came. He had shaken Amma off his feet like a dog ridding itself of fleas. "I am sorry, Naseem, but please, don't embarrass yourself," he said. "My hands are tied. I must do what is best for my son. Tell Saleem that this will not be forgotten so easily." He glanced at Nazia, then looked away. "We have no choice but to look to the village for my son's bride."

Amma wiped her face with her tearstained dupatta. "Take Nazia with you. We'll send the jahez in installments if that's what you care about."

"It's not just the dowry, Naseem," said Uncle Tariq. "Look at her. She is sickly. Her body is frail, her eyes are hollow, and her skin is darker than the dirt on the floor. And more than that, she has roamed the streets with you in the past few months, hardened herself to the gaze of the world, and tasted the money earned from her own sweat. People will find out. If Nazia continues to earn for you, it won't be long before she begins to bend you to her will. If I take her back to the village, she'll make demands on my son and turn him against me." His voice stammered at the thought. "I—I cannot tolerate that."

"She is only a child. She wouldn't even begin to know how to manipulate a husband."

"Who knows? I don't know her anymore. Saleem is not

here to make her case, and I won't let a woman—even you, Naseem—convince me of what is best for my son."

Nazia tried to console her mother. Amma held her hand firmly. "There is nothing wrong with my daughter," she said, thrusting her chin out and shaking her fist at her brother-in-law. "She's a hardworking girl. She helped her mother and did what her own father wouldn't. If you don't fulfill the arrangement, you'll regret it. Your brother's failings are not her fault."

Uncle Tariq had left after that, and moments later the landlord had arrived with the new tenants. Iqbal gave Amma and the children only an hour to clear out their belongings, forcing them to leave behind the larger furniture, the couch, and the TV, claiming that it was all owed to him since the rent was still unpaid.

Maleeha hugged Nazia as the landlord's blue truck rumbled past them, the eviction complete. Nazia watched the truck make its way alongside the cricket pitch, the tires leaving behind a trail of dust, before it merged onto the main road. She wondered what would have happened if Abbu had come home last night. Would he have been able to save their home? Would he have been able to convince Uncle Tariq that she was still a suitable bride for Salman? She tried to picture her cousin's face, but he was still only a blur in her mind. Uncle Tariq had said that Salman was eager to get married, but she wondered if he would pick another bride from the village as easily as he would choose mangoes from the market.

Maleeha pulled Nazia inside the house, where Amma sat with her mother, speaking in low tones. Maleeha's older brother, Hisham, was in the kitchen eating a banana while he read from a textbook. Isha and Mateen were watching TV with Maleeha's little brother, too young to understand the true meaning of the unexpected visit to their neighbors'. Nazia's throat tightened at the sight of Isha staring up at the screen. Why couldn't she be a few years younger, like Isha, so Amma didn't expect so much from her?

Despite their whispering, Nazia couldn't help but overhear Maleeha's mother.

"It's not any trouble. You are like a sister to me. I insist you must stay with us until you find another place."

"It's too much." Amma was crying.

Maleeha's mother shook her head. "How can it be too much? You have lost everything." She smoothed Amma's hair. "During dark times you must know your friends and turn to them. You are staying."

Maleeha caught Nazia's gaze, and the glee in her eyes was unmistakable. Only Nazia couldn't share it. She was grateful, of course, but she realized that she possessed some of her mother's pride. And it stung.

Nazia stepped from the room and hurried outside. She slipped into the alleyway behind the house and pressed herself against the wall, crying soundlessly. She had just lost the only home she'd ever known, and to think that she'd never have a place in this neighborhood again was too much to bear. She loved Maleeha and her mother for offering their home, but a trickle of shame seeped into her heart. Shame that her father couldn't save them. Shame that her brother had deserted them.

She wiped her face with the dingy dupatta and breathed more

deeply to calm herself. Cursing her brother and father didn't change their situation.

Today she and Amma had skipped their morning cleaning route to wait with Uncle Tariq for Abbu. The break from cleaning made Nazia's muscles ache, and her back was stiff. But would being bossed around by Salman and his family while she waited for Amma and Abbu to build up the jahez month by month be any better? Before Abbu's accident she would have gladly married Salman and moved to his village without a second thought. Now, standing alone behind Maleeha's house with no place to call home, she wasn't so sure.

The wedding was off, and the men in her family had shirked their responsibilities, leaving the women to fend for themselves. Whether she liked it or not, she would be there for Amma to lean on as long as she had to. They would sleep tonight at Maleeha's, and she would go with her mother to Seema's house in the morning to beg for a place to stay.

The air came alive as the call to prayer rose up. How many prayers had she missed? How many times had she been too exhausted to fulfill her duty to Allah since she'd started working? Nazia had lost count.

She walked back inside to perform wazu. This time she would pray. She would pray for Seema to let them stay on her property. There was no time to dwell on the possibilities if the memsahib refused.

"Watch out!" Nazia grabbed Mateen's arm and pulled him back as the brightly painted bus squealed past them and came to a stop along the main road near the cricket pitch. The decorative trim that hung from the window flashed under the too-bright sun and jangled together, the metallic sound competing with the Indian pop music that blared from the driver's cassette player.

Nazia handed off her whimpering brother to Amma. Nazia had snapped at him louder than she needed to, but fear of the unknown put her on edge. Maleeha had walked to the bus stop with them, and Nazia had been struggling to hold back the turmoil within her. She didn't want her best friend to know how afraid she really was. But Maleeha already knew.

"Don't worry, Nazia. Hisham and I will talk to our mother. Maybe she and Abbu can find someplace for you so you won't have to go. And you know our parents insist that you stay with us if you don't find a place. Even if your mother is too full of pride to listen, you must convince her. Our home will always be open to you."

Nazia nodded, fighting desperately to hold back the tears. She clung to Maleeha for a second longer before pulling away. "I know, Maleeha. You're the greatest friend ever."

The bus driver blasted his horn in a final warning. Nazia reached inside her backpack, pulled out a folded scrap of paper, and stuffed it into Maleeha's hand. "Keep this safe. Give it to Abbu when he returns."

Nazia followed the surge of women toward the bus, craning her neck to keep Amma in sight just ahead as she climbed the steep steps. The attendant lifted Isha and Mateen aboard, and they settled onto a bench near the driver. Nazia remained standing and held on to the back of the driver's seat for support as the bus jerked into motion. Through the open window she watched Maleeha waving good-bye and getting smaller and smaller as they pulled away. Within seconds her friend was gone, lost in the chaos of constant traffic.

Amma pulled Mateen close to her when the bus started rolling, the swaying motion forcing the passengers to lean hard against one another at every curve in the road. Nazia gripped the seat and glanced around at the other women. Where were they headed? Most were wearing the black *hijab* that covers the length of the body, revealing only their faces and their hands. Others sat with their dupattas sliding down their heads, eyes open but cast downward, and lost in a dreamland from the moment they took their seats.

The ride was short, less than ten minutes. Nazia soaked in the view of the busy market until the bus lurched to a stop in front of the meat stall where they had met Shenaz almost a month ago. She got off the bus, helped her family, then headed down the narrow alleyway where cars were parked haphazardly alongside storefronts and beggars were already making the rounds.

When they reached Seema's house, Sherzad was already by the

gate with the door swinging open before Amma could ring the buzzer. "As salam-o-alaikum!" He stood rigidly, saluting as they entered. Amma hurried silently toward the house with Isha and Mateen.

"Wa laikum as salam." Nazia brushed past him, suddenly cringing as she realized that she had forgotten to bring the boy the extra food she had promised.

"You're here early," Sherzad said. He walked alongside Nazia up the driveway and around the house to the kitchen entrance, his arms swinging loosely.

"Amma's going to ask baji for a place to stay."

Sherzad's eyes widened. "Really?"

The memory of last night bubbled up inside her. Nazia explained what had happened.

"Don't you have relatives in Karachi?" Sherzad asked.

She thought of her uncle. "No. No relatives in Karachi. My uncle lives in Punjab."

"What about your father?" Sherzad stopped at the door while Nazia removed her slippers and Amma settled Isha and Mateen on the veranda.

"We haven't seen him for two days." Where was he? What if he was lying somewhere injured and helpless? Or had he found a job where they hired him right away and he couldn't leave work to tell them he was okay? Or was he just like her brother and her uncle? Did he run away just when they needed him, too? She couldn't let herself believe that, not yet.

Amma climbed up the steps and into the kitchen. "Inside, Nazia," she called.

Nazia followed her mother into the lounge, where Seema sat on a sagging chair with her back to the kitchen, watching a cooking show on PTV. On the screen a tall Indian man with a pointy mustache diced an onion and scraped it into a steel pot, all the while moving his chef's knife floridly in the air. When Amma called out a greeting, Seema lifted a hand in acknowledgment. Amma put a finger to her lips and motioned for Nazia to follow her. They sat on the floor.

Amma and Seema talked about the weather and the price of eggs and bread. Seema was hunched in her chair. Her clothes looked wrinkled and slept in, and clumps of jet-black hair hung loosely around her face, free from the plastic hair clip that held the remaining locks in place. She sipped tea from a chipped porcelain cup, and the heady aroma made Nazia's stomach tighten. Maleeha's mother had offered them leftover rice and *parratha* for breakfast. The flatbread fried in *ghee* was devoured quickly, but there hadn't been nearly enough to satisfy the stomachs of two families. The onions cooking on the screen were joined by a dash of salt, chili powder, ginger, and garlic, and Nazia's mouth began to water.

"Why are you here so early?" Seema rested the cup on the arm of her chair.

Amma launched into the events of the past two days. Seema's eyebrows rose at the part where Uncle Tariq had called off the engagement when Abbu never showed up.

"So what will you do now?"

"Our place is occupied and they've taken our furniture, our beds. We have only a few bags and some kitchen items, which we left at a neighbor's." Amma glanced at Nazia and licked her lips, then placed a hand on Seema's foot. "You have empty rooms. We need only one since the men are gone. We won't cause you any trouble. We could help you in the evenings, whatever you like. Sherzad sleeps by the gate, and the back quarters are empty. We could clean them out and you won't even notice we are here. Please, baji. Let us stay here with you?"

"Won't notice you're here, eh?" Seema chuckled. "What about all the meals? Now I only give you and the girl lunch. If you stay, then you'll want breakfast, lunch, tea, and dinner. Who can pay for that?"

Nazia wondered the same, given how hungry Sherzad always was. How could there possibly be enough for all of them?

Amma squeezed Seema's foot, then released it to clasp her hands together. "Baji, please. We won't eat much. We'll still have the money from cleaning houses."

Seema stared thoughtfully at the TV and finished her tea.

The chef had added yogurt and plump pieces of chicken to the curry, which was now bubbling over a low flame. Nazia pressed her arms around herself to keep her stomach from grumbling.

"What about your husband?" Seema asked finally. "What would you do if he returns?"

"He won't," Amma said quickly. "He's been gone for two days, and he doesn't know where we work."

Nazia shifted uncomfortably, knowing that Maleeha kept a folded scrap of paper in her backpack to give to Abbu if she ever saw him, the address of Seema's house written in careful Urdu in Nazia's own handwriting.

"What about your son, then? You've always said he'd return to you."

Amma groaned. "My son, my husband, my brother-in-law. All the men in our family are the same. I don't know why—I guess I'll never understand it—but that's just the way it is for people like us."

"Yes," Seema agreed. "Look at Shenaz. Her husband is just as worthless, but she is not bound to him by children. Why would the lazy brutes get a job when they know they can live off the hard work of a woman?"

Nazia opened her mouth but closed it. There would be no use in defending Abbu right now. No matter what Amma or Seema thought, Nazia knew that finding a place to stay was more important. Even if that meant Amma had to bad-mouth Abbu.

"Of course! They know our women will go to any lengths to feed their children. The men know this all too well and use it against us. They suck the joy from our marrow, like leeches."

Nazia turned sharply to look at her mother. Was it really that bad for her? Was Amma so unhappy with Abbu, or was she only making a case for a place to stay? She tried to catch her mother's eye, but Amma refused to look at her.

Seema stood and pulled at her gauze-thin shalwar kameeze. "You can stay, but if your son shows up—or even your husband—they are not welcome." She picked up her teacup and headed to the kitchen. "Come. I'll show you your room."

Why couldn't Amma hold her tongue! When Amma motioned at her to get up, Nazia stood up hastily and tried not to pout. At least they had a place to stay. She knew Amma would want her to be grateful for that, so she bit the inside of her lip, grabbed her mother's arm, and squeezed it gently.

Outside, the sun was hot on the concrete that surrounded the house, and only a portion of the veranda offered shade. Mateen and Isha were lying limp on the terrace, the cool marble beneath them the only solace from the heat.

Seema stopped and waved a hand at them. "They'll look like dried-up raisins if they stay here."

"Uttoh!" Amma shouted at them. "Get up!"

Amma grabbed Isha's arm and dragged her across the smooth flooring to the shade of a concrete awning. A film of dust was swept along by the trailing end of Isha's cotton kameeze. Nazia pulled Mateen to rest alongside his sister, and her heart ached for him when he didn't even bother to open his eyes at the movement.

"Senseless kids," Amma grumbled. "Don't even have the brains to move into the shade."

"They're tired and hungry," Nazia snapped.

Seema walked toward the back of the house. A row of concrete brick shacks was built against the property wall, consisting of four rooms. The doors were made of slats nailed together, the wood old and weathered, with strips of blue paint still visible.

Seema positioned her shoulder against the first door and gave it a hard shove. The wood had expanded from years of heat and neglect, and it scraped roughly against the ground as it opened. The sunlight cut into the depths of the putrid-smelling room, and dust swirled in the air. Nazia and her mother waited outside while Seema ducked her head and entered. With one hand on her hip and the other pressing her dupatta against her mouth, she took in the dilapidated condition of the servant quarters. "We haven't had a servant living in here in ages," she said, almost apologetically. She looked around for a moment, then stepped back out into the sun and shook the dust from her dupatta. "Well, it needs work. You can clean it up when you're done with the house. It has two charpais — should be enough if you sleep two per bed. The servants' bathroom is at the end of the row down there. I'm sure it needs cleaning too."

Amma began a shower of thanks and blessed Seema for her kindness.

"Well, don't be too quick in your thanks, Naseem," Seema warned. "I'm not finished. Leave these middle two rooms alone. Sahib is using them for storage. As for food and rent, you'll get all your meals, even the children, but you'll have to forfeit the income from cleaning my house. You can still work and keep the money from the other houses, but in the evenings you'll need to help out here."

Amma must have known that she'd be asked to give up the income from Seema's house, because she didn't raise a single protest. Nazia wondered fleetingly if there would be any money left over to rebuild her dowry.

"It will be nice to have live-in servants again." Seema smiled.

"Baji, but you have Sherzad."

"Oh, he's just a boy. He can't do everything."

Amma chuckled. "Don't worry, baji. You'll be happy with us. I promise you."

Seema waved her away. "Fine, fine. I have some things you can use, old clothes, sheets, dishes. I'll sort through my things while you're working."

After Seema went back inside, Amma gave Nazia a hug. "See that? Allah is on our side."

Nazia wondered if her prayer had helped. She wrestled out of her mother's grasp. "What about Abbu?"

A frown flashed across Amma's face but was gone just as quickly. "He can take care of himself. Where was he when Iqbal threw us on the street? Where was he when his brother broke off your marriage? He'll fend for himself. I've come to realize that Bilal and your father are the same. I didn't want to believe it, but I'm not blind, you know. I see that we are alone. I see that I am carrying this family all alone."

So Amma was giving up on Abbu. A part of Nazia understood Amma's willingness to abandon Abbu, but another part of her struggled to change Amma's mind. Everything would always be so much harder for them without Abbu. Why couldn't Amma see that? Was she willing to struggle the rest of her life? Whether Amma believed it or not, they *needed* Abbu. Nazia realized that she was the only one who still believed in him and decided that from now on she'd keep her faith in Abbu to herself. She didn't want to hurt Amma, but she couldn't abandon Abbu so easily.

"Not all alone, Amma." Nazia's voice softened. "I'm here. I'm helping too, aren't I?"

Amma cupped her daughter's face in her hands. "Yes, beta. You are always here to help me. A daughter is worth a hundred sons, no matter what the rest of the world says. Come now. Let's get to work."

———— ▸◂ ————

By nightfall the air was still, and heat clung like a wet towel against Nazia's skin. She had pulled a charpai from her quarters and positioned it in the narrow passageway between the main house and the boundary wall in the hopes of resting in the steady breeze that came from the sea.

Except for the drone of the neighbor's generator to combat the blackouts caused by load shedding, the air was still. The electricity had gone out immediately after *Khabarnama*, the evening news. Nazia supposed the temporary blackouts were planned and announced in newspapers, but since her mother rarely had the money to spare on a newspaper, the electrical outages were always an unwelcome surprise. Seema and the sahib had gone to Clifton Beach for the evening to escape the stifling heat. Only Sherzad sat outside the front gate, guarding the house.

"Sit still, Isha." Nazia gathered her sister's hair in one hand and ran a comb through the oiled mass to smooth out the tangles before she braided it.

"You're hurting me." Isha tried to pull away.

Nazia gave her sister's hair a quick jerk. "If you don't stop moving, I'm gonna tell Amma and she'll cut it all off."

Isha leaped off the charpai, then whirled back to look at Nazia. "And I'm going to tell Amma that you're hurting me on purpose!" She covered her mouth with shaky fingers.

Nazia immediately felt sorry. "Well, don't cry about it." She held out her arms. "Come back and let me finish. I promise I'll be gentle."

Isha looked at her sister skeptically.

"I said I promise."

Isha edged closer, and Nazia pulled her onto the charpai. She wrapped her arms around her sister and kissed her on both cheeks. "What will I do when you get too old to boss around?"

"I don't want to get old."

"You can't stop it, *chotti*."

Isha curled up against Nazia. "I want to stay with you forever."

"Well, you have to stop that thinking right now. What will you do when I'm off and married?"

"Take me with you?"

"No," Nazia said slowly. "You'll have your own family to go to when the time comes."

Isha pulled away again. "No! I'll stay with Amma and Mateen. You can stay too, if you want. You just don't want to be with us anymore. You want to run away, just like Abbu and Bilal bhai."

"That's not true!" Nazia protested. "Why would I want to leave all of you? My life was planned when I was younger than you, chotti. No one asked me what I wanted." How could she explain the traditions of matrimony to her sister when she barely understood the cultural requirements herself?

Amma had never sat her down and explained what would happen in all the years of growing up. Anything that happened in their lives was always seen as inevitable, as Allah's will. There was never any room in their tiny existence to entertain the possibility of other choices, other dreams.

Isha struggled to keep her voice full of fury, but her eyes

brimmed with tears. "Well, I hope you never get the money for the dowry."

Nazia looked at her sharply. "How can you say that?"

"Because then you'll have to stay with us forever," she said.

Nazia waved the comb at Isha, who returned to the edge of the charpai and glumly allowed her hair to be braided.

How would they save any extra money to build up a dowry? Nazia twisted her sister's hair and tied the end with a strip of cloth. Without the money from Seema baji, they would have to find another house to clean. But that would be more than Amma's tired body could handle. No, they'd have to find another way.

She moved off the charpai and began taking down the clothes that she had washed earlier from the line. Mixed in with their own worn-out cotton shalwar kameezes were outdated embroidered outfits that Seema baji had dug out from storage. Despite the fact that the beadwork was tarnished and the coloring from the intricately patterned threads had bled and permanently stained the shiny material, the garments were still beautiful.

Nazia recalled the way her mother had taken the used clothes from Seema and hung her head in gratitude. Nazia had fought hard to squelch the fury that had rushed up inside her as she remembered the dowry garments, brand new and modeled after the latest fashion trends in the glossy magazines, far more exquisite than the baji's hand-me-downs. How had things gotten so irrevocably bad?

But it's not irrevocable, Nazia thought suddenly. She yanked at the clothes, letting the clothespins fall carelessly to the ground. They wouldn't have to clean houses forever if only Nazia could find another way to make more money. She had skills. She could sew, she could cook, clean, care for children. She could read and write.

She carried the pile of clothes back into their quarters and dropped them on the remaining charpai, where her mother and Mateen lay sleeping. Nazia had noticed that there were many other children who accompanied their mothers and sisters as they roamed the streets going from house to house on their own jobs cleaning, cooking, or doing whatever else the wealthy residents of Defence required. Would those mothers be willing to pay her if she taught their children how to read and write? Many couldn't care less, she knew, given how they all seemed to struggle for every rupee. But some would, especially for their sons. She shook out the wrinkles and folded the clothes into a neat pile. One way or another she would find a way to make some extra money.

Isha's words crept into her thoughts. *You can stay too, if you want.* For the first time she wondered if she really did have a choice. *Could* she stay with her family forever? She didn't know the answer, but at least when the time came, she'd make sure she had the means to support whatever the future held for her. She knew only that she didn't want to live like Amma, being swept away by whatever wind blew over her.

She put the clothes inside a sheet, crossed the ends, and tied them together. She went back out and crawled onto the ropes of the charpai, covering Isha and herself with her dupatta. Amma wouldn't like it that she slept out in the open and would scold her in the morning. But Amma was asleep and the air was too stifling in the quarters. *Amma will just have to understand,* she thought. There were times when silly rules had to be broken. And this was one of them, she thought, grateful for the sudden breeze that kicked up and rushed through the passageway. She breathed in the salty air and gazed up at the stars for a long time before drifting off to sleep.

Nazia tightened her grip on the bat and tapped the squared-off end on the ground. Sweating hard, she looked up at the bowler and squinted to keep the glare of the noon sun out. The bowler was laughing at her. She wiped the sweat from her eyes to get a better look at the him. It was her brother Bilal. The crowd behind her began chanting her name. Bilal's laughter ceased abruptly, and he threw the ball.

Nazia swung hard. The pitch came in low, but the ball connected and the crack of the bat reverberated throughout the field. She clutched the bat and ran toward the wicket, but her brother threw the ball to the wicketkeeper before she could reach it. She stopped short when she saw who had caught the ball. It was Abbu. Her father punched the air with a fist and pointed at her. "You're out, chotti! You're out."

The crowd began to rush the pitch, and Amma led the charge straight at her. Nazia dropped to the ground, covering her head with her hands. Their chanting swelled, and even though she pressed her palms against her ears, she couldn't block out the terrifying sounds. "You're out! Get out! You're out! Get out!" The yelling intensified as the crowd grew and was accompanied by the hard pounding of cricket bats against the earth, thumping an angry rhythm whose beat rose high above the playing field. The thumping grew louder and louder until Nazia felt as though they were beating the bats against her head.

Nazia awoke with a start, bumping her head against the bamboo side of the charpai. The door to the servant quarters was rattling, and the fervent banging continued.

"Get up!" The door rattled again.

She shook away the dream and rose unsteadily off the rickety bed, trying to keep from waking Isha. Halfway through the night Amma had shaken her awake and demanded that she move the charpai into the servant quarters.

The thumping came again. "I'm coming!" she whispered.

Nazia opened the door a crack and peered out. It was barely dawn, and the sky still held the bluish-gray hue of night. Sherzad stood glaring at her, his feet bare and his hair tousled. "What's got you up so early?" she mumbled.

"Are you deaf? I've been banging on the door forever! You sleep like the dead in there."

"Well, maybe you weren't knocking hard enough." She didn't think her dream was any of his business.

"Was so." He crossed his arms and let his hands rest in his armpits. "Okay, maybe not. He told me not to wake your mother."

Nazia rubbed her eyes and yawned. "Who told you that?"

"Your abbu."

"My abbu?"

"He's outside the gate. He told me to come get you, so could you hurry up so I can get some sleep before baji wakes up?"

Fully alert now, Nazia hurried to the gate. Abbu probably had come home, only to find his family gone and strangers sitting on their sofa. Maleeha must have given him the address to Seema's place. The next time she saw Maleeha, she'd have to remember to thank her for sending Abbu to her.

She lifted the lever carefully to keep the iron latch from squeaking, slid the lock back, pushed open the gate, and slipped onto the street. Her heart stilled when she saw her father.

Abbu rushed to wrap his arms around her, engulfing her small frame in the folds of his shirt. Nazia's feet left the ground and the sky whirled above her as he swung her around in his strong grip. She breathed in the sweat and stench of her father's filthy clothes, but she didn't care and clung to him tightly. He'd been gone only three days, but Nazia felt as if she'd trekked across the desert in his absence.

"Nazia! Chotti! I'm so glad to see you. Let me look at you." He cocked his head and smiled at her. "You've grown so much."

Nazia giggled. "I have not."

"Of course you have," he said in mock seriousness. "A child can grow into a woman in the blink of an eye!"

"Abbu, I'm not a woman." Nazia stopped laughing. "And I don't want to be."

"Okay, beta. You'll always be my little chotti." He grabbed her by the shoulders and shook her gently. "Now, stop being so serious. You look so much like your mother, you're frightening me!" He let go of her and pretended to bite his dirt-encrusted fingernails.

Nazia couldn't help but laugh at his antics. She couldn't

remember the last time she had laughed. She was certain, though, that it had to have been with Abbu. She sighed. Even though she didn't want to end the silly moment, there were questions to ask and problems to solve.

She froze his smiling face in her mind and locked it away for safekeeping. She watched his short mustache wiggle as he pretended to bite his nails. His teeth were straight but deeply stained from the juice of betel leaves and roadside tea. The skin around his eyes crinkled up as he laughed, and his cheeks puffed out like baby potatoes. Nazia was surprised by the glimpse of Abbu as he used to be before the accident, and she cherished the moment, glad that they were alone.

"It won't be long before you go back to the village. I'll give you and Salman a wedding the village will talk about for years to come!"

She inhaled deeply. Someone had to tell him. It might as well be her. "There's not going to be a wedding," Nazia said. "At least not with Salman."

Abbu looked confused, and Nazia launched into the tale of her uncle's visit, the canceled wedding, the eviction, and the search for a place to live.

Sherzad came through the gate. "Baji's coming!" He disappeared again, but they could hear his voice as he tried to steer Seema back to the house.

Abbu grabbed Nazia's arms, and she bit back the wince as his fingernails dug into her flesh.

"Listen to me, chotti. We don't have much time."

"*Gee*, Abbu."

His face was solemn. "I need to stay here with you. Do whatever you must to convince baji to let me stay. Can you do that for me?"

Nazia nodded slowly. "I'll ask her. But she already told Amma that if you or Bilal bhai come, she won't let you stay."

"That's where I need your help, chotti. You have to convince her. I have no place else to go. If everything is as you say, then I can't go back to Punjab until we have your dowry. I've spent all this time looking for work and found nothing. I need a place to rest and regain my strength to work again."

"But you are fine now, right? You said so yourself when you went to see Iqbal about the rent. And you aren't limping anymore."

"You are right, chotti. I am fine, but there's no work. Maybe your baji or the baji's sahib has something I can do here, a mali, a chowkidar, anything."

"Sherzad, the boy you met, does all the other work around here, including the gardening and the gatekeeping. I don't think there's any work here for you, Abbu."

His face fell, and he looked away. From the other side of the wall Sherzad's and baji's voices were coming closer.

"But I'll ask the baji," she said. "Even if there isn't any work here, maybe you can still stay here. And the sahib may have something. Who knows? I'm sure the baji wouldn't want to split up a family."

"That's my girl. Now, don't tell Amma that I asked you to do this for me. You know how upset she gets when she doesn't believe I've done enough. She cleans a few houses, pulls my children out of school, and all of a sudden she thinks she's a man."

Nazia ignored his sharp words and snaked her arms around his waist for a quick hug before hurrying back to the gate, where she could hear the latch being lifted. Just as she was about to slip inside, Seema baji stepped through the small gate and out onto the street.

The memsahib's gaze swung from Nazia to her father. "As salam-o-alaikum," she said in a haughty tone.

"Wa laikum as salam," Nazia said carefully. Abbu stepped forward to return the greeting. He alternately bowed his head and puffed out his chest in an effort to impress the rumpled memsahib.

Seema's kameeze was wrinkled and her shalwar clung to her legs. Her hair was tied up in a rubber band, accentuating the sagging skin and the lines of her face. She placed her hands on her hips. "Who is this?"

Nazia smiled eagerly. "Abbu came to see us. To make sure we were okay."

"I see your leg is better now." Seema baji bent down to pick up a bit of debris in front of her boundary wall. Sherzad was beside her immediately and snatched the trash from her fingers.

"Gee, baji," Abbu replied hastily. "I've been all over Karachi searching for work. My legs ache like an old man's, so I thought I'd visit my family, maybe rest here for the day if you'll allow it."

"Baji, please," interjected Nazia. "Isha and Mateen would cry their hearts out if they knew Abbu came here and didn't even stay to see them. Please."

Seema stared at her for a long moment, then abruptly turned and walked the length of her property alongside the road, picking up errant paper, plastic shopping bags blown up against the wall, and fallen leaves from a neighboring neem tree. Sherzad followed her every movement like a puppy, waiting with outstretched arms whenever she picked up another bit of trash. Finally she spoke.

"Naseem is very unhappy with you," she said to Abbu.

"I know." Abbu dropped his shoulders and stared at the ground. "It's understandable, I suppose. Once a man loses a good job, it's hard to find another in this city. There's maybe one job for every five hundred men. My weary feet say maybe worse."

Seema gave him a sour look and shook her head. "You men are all so much alike. Always an excuse." She wagged a finger at him. "You have no job now because Naseem works. Your daughter works. You've tasted the money of a desperate mother, and now you've learned how to keep the water flowing. When the well runs dry, disappear. Naseem and Nazia will work harder. More water will come. You all know the game so well; I don't understand why Naseem bothers to share any of it with you."

"You are wrong, baji, I'm not——"

"Abbu's not that way, baji!" Nazia cried.

Seema shot Nazia a hard look. "Don't you fall for your father's lies. He'll do anything to get someone on his side."

"You don't know him." Nazia jutted her chin out. "You only know Amma's story, not his."

"I know your engagement is over. I know you don't go to school. I know your mother works until she's near dead every day for you kids. All that is your father's fault."

Nazia's eyes filled with tears. Everything Seema said was true, but did it mean that her father had to go away? That they would have to clean houses forever or at least until someone decided to marry her? She stared at the memsahib, realizing that if Abbu left, she would never be a little girl again. A small cry escaped her lips, and she slapped a hand against her mouth, stifling the fear.

Seema rubbed a hand on her back. "Oh, fine. Don't say I didn't warn you. Hush. Stop your crying." She started toward the gate. "He can stay for now, but there's no work here. Sherzad is more than enough for me." She turned to Abbu. "I'll check with the sahib and see if he has any work. Now get in here. Nazia has work to do."

Amma came toward the gate. "Why did you let him in?"

Seema shrugged as she headed back inside. "Your daughter. She begged me."

Nazia pretended not to hear their exchange. She pulled her father inside, closing the gate door behind them. Why did Amma have to make a big commotion about everything? She'd settled it already, hadn't she?

"Don't close that gate!" Amma shouted, pushing Nazia aside. She threw the latch open and tried to force Abbu back out.

"Amma! What are you doing?"

Amma pounded Abbu's chest. "You let your own daughter beg for you? You don't care about her. You don't care about any of us!"

Nazia pulled at Amma, but it was Abbu who easily held Amma at arm's length to keep from getting bombarded by her blows.

Nazia squeezed herself between them. "Stop it, both of you! Just stop it!"

Amma yanked her arms from Abbu's grip and looked at Nazia, her chest heaving. "You two deserve each other. Both of you, nothing but dreamers!"

Nazia dropped her shoulders in dismay. "Don't say that, Amma!"

"Dreaming doesn't put food on the table or a roof over your head."

Abbu held out a hand and tried to smooth Amma's hair, but she swatted him away. "Please, just listen to me," he said. "I've been all over the city looking for work. I—"

"I don't believe you!" Amma's eyes were venomous.

Nazia wrapped her arms around Amma. She whispered into the folds of her neck and her sweaty hair. "Amma, give him another chance. Seema said she will ask the sahib if he has work for him. He just needs another chance!"

"He doesn't deserve another chance!" Amma spat near his feet, but Nazia only tightened her grip.

"Just once."

Finally, after a few minutes, when Amma's breathing became easier and her body sagged against Nazia, Amma relented.

"Fine," she muttered. "Let the coward stay." Amma pulled away and looked Nazia in the eye. "But it will only be a matter of days before we'll regret it."

Abbu pulled them apart before Nazia could reply. He embraced them both, surrounding them with words of relief, nervous laughter, and a promise that he would work hard.

Nazia wondered fleetingly if Amma was right, if they would regret letting Abbu return so easily. She hoped not, but she couldn't dwell on it either, because the younger ones had heard Abbu's voice in all the commotion. They came running, their innocent faces full of joy.

Seema convinced the sahib to employ Abbu at one of his construction sites in the city. As an investment developer, he bought land in and around Karachi, erecting factories and plants. He also worked with architects to construct modern houses, which Pakistanis returning from abroad and other countries' expatriates would prefer to live in.

Amma had simmered for some time when she realized that Abbu intended to stay at the servant quarters rather than find the family a real home. And why wouldn't he? Nazia had reasoned. There was no rent to pay and the food was part of the deal, except for Abbu, who had to buy his meals from the roadside stalls in Defence Market. Isha and Mateen were elated that Abbu was nearby and they no longer had to worry about their missing father.

Abbu went to the construction site every day and returned nightly. Amma and Nazia continued to clean the other two houses during the day and returned in the afternoons to Seema's place. Seema baji had even given Isha and Mateen small duties around the house, such as watering the outdoor plants, weeding the garden, and sifting through rice and lentils.

Amma had gotten Seema to let them clean out the adjacent room to make room for Abbu, and Isha and Mateen made a game every night of choosing which room to sleep in.

Nazia managed to pick up some sewing from an embroidery shop down in the market, next to the tailor who made custom-fitted shalwar suits. The shopkeeper sold dupattas and an array of lace and trim. He received numerous requests to sew the trim directly onto the dupattas, and he met the demand by operating sewing machines in his shop to keep up with the orders. But other ladies often came in with their own clothes, asking for size alterations, rips to be repaired, and lace to be added.

The shopkeeper had been impressed with Nazia's initiative and had been pleased to offer to pay her a small fee for the work she took home and brought back the next day. It wasn't long before he began relying on her punctual appearance every afternoon before teatime to pick up more work, and then deliver the finished garments the following day before midday prayers.

Nazia was careful not to spend the money she earned from the sewing on anything, and even Amma didn't ask her about it. Slowly but surely the money she stashed in a rusty container beneath a pile of old newspapers was growing.

One day Seema held a dinner party for the sahib's friends and business associates. The sahib had expanded the guest list without telling the memsahib, so Seema spent the day tiring out Sherzad, Nazia, Amma, and even Isha as they washed, cleaned, mopped, dusted, and ran to the market to buy last-minute items such as yogurt and milk.

Sherzad had been sick all day with a high fever, and yet he managed to run the grass cutter and trim the bushes before collapsing in his room after lunch. While he slept, Nazia covered for him and did the remainder of the work herself. The memsahib had been upset that Sherzad had fallen ill on the day of an important party, but Nazia insisted that she'd do his work. "There's plenty of work to go around," the memsahib had replied, and insisted that Sherzad be prepared to work again once the party got under way.

At half past nine the Khabarnama evening news ended, and guests began to trickle in. The chicken *tikka*, meatball *qorma*, lamb-and-rice *biryani*, and potato-and-cauliflower sauté were all ready. Only the garnishing and yogurt *raita* remained. Nazia stood at the island in the kitchen and diced onions and cilantro to mix into the yogurt.

The sahib hobbled into the kitchen. "Where is everyone? Doesn't anyone hear the buzzer?"

Seema began pulling out serving bowls from the cupboard. "I'm sure Sherzad is around here somewhere. I thought he was in the back bringing out more chairs. Or maybe he's at the market. I gave him money to buy the bread."

"He should be at the gate. We can't have the guests standing out on the street waiting."

Seema set the bowls on the island and began wiping out the dust with a damp cloth. "Nazia, get the door. Leave the latch open so guests can enter on their own, then go look for Sherzad." She glanced at the sahib. "Good enough?"

"What's the point of having so many servants if there's none when you need them?" He stamped his cane on the floor.

Nazia scooped the diced onions into the bowl of yogurt and

then quickly washed her hands at the sink while she listened to the exchange.

"Where's Saleem?" Seema asked her husband. "Didn't Nazia's father come back with you?"

"We just had a shipment of supplies, and the chowkidar had to leave. So I asked Saleem to stay and guard the materials."

"Couldn't you have asked someone else? You knew about this party — it would help to have him here tonight."

"His entire family is here, the boy is here, how many servants could you possibly need for the party?"

"Sherzad is ill today. Even if Nazia finds him, I'm not sure he'll be of much use tonight."

The buzzer sounded long and hard, interrupting their argument. They both turned to Nazia.

"Are you still here?" shouted Seema.

Nazia pushed open the kitchen door and dashed down the steps. She ran barefoot around the house and down the driveway to unlatch the gate, then stepped aside to let the guests in.

A tall man dressed in trousers brushed past her, followed by a thin woman who gave Nazia a haughty look. They spat out words at her, but Nazia didn't understand them. She realized they were speaking in English.

Nazia ducked her head, apologizing in Urdu, as they marched toward the house, where the sahib stood, holding open the front door. For the next few minutes a steady stream of finely dressed guests passed through the gates. Their cars lined the street, and drivers gathered outside across the street, chatting and milling about while their passengers were entertained.

Nazia waited for a lull in the line of people that trickled through, and then peeped inside Sherzad's room to check on him. He was curled up on the charpai, his eyes closed and his arms wrapped around his stomach. "Sherzad?" The boy didn't move, but a low moan escaped his lips. She called his name again as she stepped into the dank quarters.

He moaned, the guttural sound sending a chill down her spine. She touched his arm, then recoiled, alarmed by his burning-hot skin. "Sherzad! You have a fever!" She touched his forehead with the palm of her hand. "You must get to the doctor."

He tried to speak, but his lips were parched.

"Should I get baji?"

He licked his lips. "No," Sherzad mumbled. "Just sleep."

Nazia could hear the sounds of more guests coming through the iron gate, their laughter loud and high-pitched. The party was in full swing, and Nazia knew she had to get back to help Seema in the kitchen.

"Let me get Amma. Maybe she can help you." When the boy didn't reply, Nazia tucked the flimsy blanket that lay at the foot of the charpai around his frail body. "I'll be right back," she promised.

She ran back to the bustling kitchen. Amma was at the counter pouring ice-cold water into glasses on a tray. Seema was ladling food into the serving dishes, and a number of the guests were milling about, watching.

"Baji," Nazia began, "Sherzad is —"

Seema whirled about, her face pinched. "Where have you been? I send you to open the gate and you completely disappear. Where's Sherzad?"

"He's sick, baji. He's burning with fever."

"You tell him to go get the naan. He should have been back by now with the bread. Everything will be cold now if we wait for him."

"But baji, he can't move," Nazia implored. "Can't you ask one of the drivers to get it?"

Seema slapped Nazia hard. Nazia's hands flew to her stinging cheek, and she stumbled until her back hit the edge of the counter. She stared at the memsahib, her eyes smarting. Amma held the water pitcher in midair. The guests went on talking, taking no notice of the incident.

"Don't you ever tell me how to run my house." Seema shot Amma a quick look, then turned back to Nazia. "You'd better teach your daughter to know her place, Naseem. Or there will be no place for her here."

"Gee, baji," Amma mumbled. "She's only worried about the boy."

"She'd better only worry about herself."

Amma lowered her gaze and turned back to pouring water slowly into the remaining glasses.

"Go drag that boy from his room and bring him to me."

"Baji, he can't move." Nazia's voice trembled.

Seema's face reddened as she threw off her apron, revealing a pale-blue chiffon kameeze with silver beadwork glittering across the bodice. The delicate fabric swirled around her as she grabbed Nazia's arm and dragged her out the side door. Nazia bit back a yelp when she stubbed her bare toe as she stumbled down the kitchen steps.

Nazia ran alongside Seema baji to keep from being dragged on the walk as they made their way to the front of the house. A lamp tied to an overhead electric line illuminated the lawn, where chairs were set up to accommodate the men who preferred to stay outdoors. Every chair was taken, and many men stood in clumps laughing, their voices filling the air with a steady hum. Children ran, weaving among the bamboo chairs, their play spilling over into the driveway.

Seema slowed, walking stiffly past the guests so as not to attract their attention. When she reached the small room beside the gate, she released Nazia and strode in to find Sherzad sitting up, holding his head.

Nazia watched as the memsahib grabbed the boy's thin wrists and yanked him from the charpai. Sherzad's eyes fluttered open. He stumbled and caught himself, then stepped onto the driveway, his body swaying slightly.

"Didn't I tell you to get the bread?" Seema's voice was low and harsh. "Where's the money I gave you? Answer me!" She shook his shoulders. "You could have at least given the money to one of the drivers to fetch the naan if you were so sick."

Nazia saw a few of the guests watching them casually.

Sherzad mumbled something that only made the memsahib more furious.

"Just give me the money back, you idiot. I'll send someone else." She tugged at Sherzad's shirt, trying to pull the wadded-up rupees from his pocket. Sherzad moaned and suddenly doubled over to vomit. The vomit spewed all over the bottom of Seema's new shalwar. She screamed as the vomit fell onto her sandals and slipped between her toes.

Nazia grabbed Sherzad, bearing his weight as he slumped against her. He clung to her while she helped him back into his room and laid him on the bed. When she was sure he wouldn't be sick again, she grabbed his blanket and dashed outside to wipe the putrid bile off the baji's clothes.

Seema screamed again, this time gaining the attention of everyone in the yard. Nazia could hear the gasps from the crowd, but all she could see was baji's red face and her bulging eyes. "Get away from me!" Nazia stepped back before the memsahib could strike her again.

Seema stumbled back to the house while Nazia stood in the driveway, unsure of what to do. Should she see if Sherzad was okay, or should she follow the baji? She knew that Seema would send someone's driver to get the bread and that Sherzad's vomit proved that he really was sick. Nothing more would be expected of him tonight. He would be left alone to sleep in peace while the party raged on.

Nazia washed her hands in the outside basin. Thankfully, none of the vomit had splashed on her. For the rest of the evening she worked in the kitchen, washing, serving, and answering to the beck and call of every guest. Long after the last one departed, Nazia worked late into the night beside her mother, cleaning up the house in the aftermath of the party. By the time she was finished, Nazia was too tired to eat the succulent food that had been set aside for the servants.

She carried her plate of rice, chicken tikka, and sautéed cauliflower along with a glass of warm cola to Sherzad's room. Empty chairs, dirty glasses, and discarded paper napkins were strewn across the yard. As she passed the debris, she made a note to herself to clean it up before she went to bed — it would be one less thing that the servant boy would get scolded for tomorrow.

Sherzad was staring up at the ceiling and lying on the charpai, an arm and a leg hanging carelessly off the bed. Nazia stayed by his door. "Brought you some food."

He did not look at her. "So many stars out tonight," he murmured. "Have you noticed?"

Nazia peered up at the dark ceiling and wondered if he'd lost his mind. "I'm in no mood to play."

Sherzad finally tore his gaze away from the ceiling and looked at her. "Come see." Gingerly he moved to the far edge of the bed, where the bamboo frame pressed up against the wall. A fine stream of crumbling cement fell like loose sand onto his kurta, and he brushed it away. "You can see the stars through the hole in the roof. There's no light in here, so they shine even brighter."

Nazia wanted to ask how anything could look brighter or more wondrous from such a dismal vantage point. Instead she put the plate on the ground and entered the cramped room. She sat on the edge of the bamboo frame and craned her neck upward, seeing nothing but blackness.

"You can't see it from there. You have to scoot down a bit."

Nazia glanced at him. His fever had broken. His hair was matted with sweat, and his shirt stuck to his chest. The air in the room was still, and she wondered how he survived sleeping in the dark, alone, night after night with no one to comfort him. She placed a hand on his forehead and was glad that his skin felt cool. "You cold?" She looked about for his blanket, then stopped when she remembered that she had used it earlier to wipe the vomit from the memsahib's shalwar.

He shook his head.

She ran a hand across her cheek, recalling the stinging slap she'd received when she had tried to tell Seema that Sherzad was sick. The boy didn't know what she had endured in order to find him help. One of the guests — a doctor — had eventually taken pity on him and informed the sahib of Sherzad's condition. The sahib had immediately given him the medicine to reduce the fever.

Nazia lay back on the knotty bed, her head pressed close to the boy's. He was so small that she wanted to curl him up against her the way she did with Isha every night. She pushed aside the thought and looked straight up to the ceiling, where a brilliant display of celestial magic played out in the gaping hole of the corrugated tin roof.

The opening had been deliberately cut, the malleable metal bent up and out to make a private window. A beam that held the roof in place blocked the view from the doorway, and she imagined that whoever had cut the opening — Sherzad himself? one of his predecessors? — had taken that small but important fact into consideration.

"It's beautiful." She struggled with her thoughts before finally summoning up the courage to ask the question that had swirled around her mind for days. "Why do you stay here?"

He shrugged. "No choice."

"But where's your family?"

"My amma and abbu live near the railway station. My *dadi* lives in Punjab." His voice was soft at the thought of his father's mother. "My brothers and sisters are spread out from Clifton Beach to beyond Zainab Market. Don't know exactly where. We haven't all been together in a long time."

His words tumbled around Nazia. She couldn't imagine being his age, her little sister's age, growing up among strangers. An image of her older brother flashed in her mind, a smiling brother who used to play cricket with her and help her with her homework. Could Bilal see the stars from wherever he lay tonight?

"Why does everyone live apart?"

"You know how it is. Your brother's gone. Your abbu is back. Families split to earn a living. My amma promised baji that I would stay here for three full harvest seasons before I could go home."

"Three years?" she asked. "They pay you to work here; they can't force you to stay."

Sherzad snorted. "I may be younger than you, but I've been doing this a lot longer than you have."

"You can leave anytime."

Sherzad sat up and hugged his knees close to his chest. "It's not the memsahib that makes me stay. It's my amma. Amma bound each of her children to one family or another, so that she always has money coming in. She spends her time going from one house to the next all around the city, collecting our pay."

How could a mother do that to her own children? Didn't she realize how badly Sherzad was being treated? Who knew how the others lived? "How many of you are there?" Nazia asked.

"Seven. Four sisters and three brothers, including me."

"Are you the youngest?"

"Of course not." He puffed out his chest the same way he had done on the first day they met. "I've two sisters—babies—younger than me."

"Are they with your mother?"

"No. The babies stay with my dadi in Punjab. But when they are old enough, Amma will bring them to the city to work."

"Not all ammas are as cruel and selfish as yours. I bet if you asked your mother, she'd let you find work near her."

He rested his chin on his knees. "Yes they are, Nazia. All mothers are that cruel. Look at baji. She's an amma. She's so mean that all her kids have grown up and run away. None of them come to visit, not even the ones still in Pakistan."

That was true. Seema baji always talked about her children and what a great success they were in all corners of the world, but not one ever came to visit, and only rarely did an operator patch through a telephone call from outside the country.

"Well, you haven't known many good women, Sherzad. Look at my mother. She would never hand us to strangers to feed herself."

"No? All the mothers want to marry off the girls so they can get rid of you and have one less mouth to feed."

"My mother's not like that!" Nazia sat up. "She's not trying to get rid of me. She just wants to see me settled and happy."

Sherzad laughed. "I have two older sisters. Amma married them both in Punjab. One of them lives just outside of Multan. She works in the fields, tends to the goats, and cares for her husband's entire family. The other is barely older than you. She stays at a *haveli* and looks after the children from the *sarkar*'s other wives. None of them are happy. Nobody cares if you're happy."

Nazia suddenly remembered Shenaz. Had she cared for her husband's other wife and their children before deciding that she'd rather be free of them?

"We all follow whatever path our mothers have laid out for us," Sherzad continued. "We all do whatever our ammas tell us, just like you do."

What if he was right? Amma had pulled her out of school and

forced her to work with her. Now that her engagement had fallen through, was Amma relieved to have her daughter with her for a few more months, or was she worried about how to get rid of her? She pushed aside the thought, unwilling to believe that her own mother could ever become as cruel and heartless as Sherzad's. She scooted off the charpai and stepped out of the room. The plate of food in the driveway was cold, but she retrieved it anyway and set it on Sherzad's charpai. "Eat this. You need to build up your strength after the fever."

Without a word the boy began shoveling the food into his mouth with his fingers. Nazia headed to the lawn to clean up the debris. In the distance a bicycle guard's shrill whistle blew strong, then trailed off into nothingness as he pedaled away down the street. While she picked up the shredded napkins and discarded glasses, a single thought nagged her. Why had Amma turned away and done nothing when Seema had slapped her?

Shafts of sunlight pierced between the wooden slats of the door and penetrated deep into the servant quarters. A sharp rapping sound woke Nazia, and she groaned, feeling the stiff muscles in her arms and shoulders protest as she stretched.

The door banged open and late-morning sunlight flooded the room. She shielded her eyes until they adjusted to the intense light, and squinted at the figure in the doorway.

"Wake up, Nazia. You've had enough sleep to last a week." Amma moved into the room and patted her shoulder. "Get up."

Despite the fact that the room was already stifling, a wave of air even more humid enveloped Nazia like a wet sheet. She groaned again as Amma helped her sit up. "I hardly slept," she mumbled.

"Go wash, and do it quickly. Seema is taking you to the Sunday bazaar." Amma lifted the rumpled sheet and folded it before tossing it onto the foot of the bed.

Nazia rubbed the sleep from her eyes. Seema always took Sherzad to the bazaar. Was the baji regretting her behavior last night and allowing the boy a day's rest?

She kissed her mother and slipped into her *chappals* before hurrying to the washroom. She smoothed her hair and kept the same clothes, remembering that the Sunday bazaar was held in an open field where the wind lifted up the tethered tents in waves and sand swept through the bazaar in swirls.

When she reached the front gate, Amma handed her two hundred rupees and ran through a list of items for Nazia to buy for the family. As she listened, she noticed that the door to Sherzad's room was closed. How could he sleep with the door closed? He would die in the heat. She moved to open it, but Amma grabbed her arm.

"He's not there."

Nazia looked at her. "What?"

"He's not there," she repeated. "That's why baji is taking you. He ran away."

Nazia smiled. "Good for him!" She leaned closer to her mother. "We talked last night. I'm sure he went to ask his mother if he could stay with her."

"Did you tell him to run away?"

"Of course not! He's not a slave, Amma. He should be allowed to come and go as he pleases." She told her about how Sherzad's mother had practically sold him to baji. "I told him that he should ask his mother if he could live with her. Maybe she could find him work close by."

Nazia's mother shook her head. "You have no business interfering with that boy's life. He knows no other way of living."

"But I only wanted him to see that not all mothers are as mean as his."

"You are giving him hope for a life that is not his fate."

"How can you know what his fate holds?"

"Nazia, don't push me. He's too young to see beyond the present. If you force him, then he can never be happy no matter where he is."

"What are you talking about? He has a right to hope for something better. Do you think I want to spend the rest of my life cleaning houses? I hope for something better too, Amma. So should you."

"All you can hope for is to get married to a good man and pray that he treats you well. That is your fate."

"That is your fate for me. What if I want something different?"

Amma's fingers dug into Nazia's flesh. "What else could you possibly want? You've always known how your life would be. Don't start thinking too much, or I warn you, you will be responsible for your own unhappiness just as you will be responsible for ruining Sherzad's life. His mother put him here for a reason. She knows what is best for him."

Nazia jerked her arm away from Amma and stalked off to gather the baskets. Before Amma had pulled her out of school,

Nazia would have believed everything that her mother said or did without a second thought. But things were different now. Amma was doing what she thought she had to do to keep them fed and warm at night, but was it the right thing to do?

When did Nazia have the right to start thinking on her own? Was there some unwritten law that said even when things were going wrong, when the choices that her parents made led to one disaster after another, she had to ride the waves, holding her breath? Even if it meant being pulled in by their reckless current, never knowing when or where she would surface?

Seema stepped outside, already fanning herself. With the sahib using their only car, Seema had borrowed the neighbor's driver to take them to the market. Nazia grabbed the baskets and slipped into the backseat next to Seema. As Amma closed the gate behind them and the driver pulled away, Nazia prayed that Sherzad's mother would welcome him home and that the little boy would never return. Her fingers twisted around the basket handles, surprised at the boy's boldness. At least he had the courage to choose his own road.

The bazaar was spread out on a large tract of barren land north of the housing development. Green canvas sheeting tied to bamboo poles offered some respite from the blazing sun, but the sand still whipped through the tents with every gust of wind.

The driver stayed with the car, too high up on the servant scale to help carry bags for a baji who was not his own. Nazia carried the baskets through the maze of stalls while Seema haggled with the vendors to cut the prices on potatoes, garlic, and tomatoes. It wasn't long before both baskets were full and the weight was almost too much for Nazia to bear. As the midday heat permeated the bazaar, her feet slowed and her head began to ache.

A group of Afghani boys in brown kurtas and bare feet trailed after them, begging to help carry the baskets.

A particularly persistent boy with dirty blond hair and hazel eyes, just barely taller than herself, tugged at the basket on her aching shoulder.

"Baji, *mazdoor?*" he asked, his eyes sparkling.

Nazia longed to say yes, but Seema baji smacked his hand away.

"We can carry it ourselves." Seema yanked up her dupatta and wiped it over her grim face.

"Baji, you are not carrying them," the boy said mildly, and turned to Nazia. "The girl is."

"That's what she's here for, you imbecile. If I wanted to pay a mazdoor, why would I have brought her along?"

"I will carry them for you for free, baji. Don't pay me."

"Are you trying to insult me?" Seema narrowed her eyes.

"No, baji." He laughed. "It's just that the baskets are heavy and the girl will break her arms by the time you are finished. Let me carry them, and I will save her arms from falling off so she can work for you longer. I won't take any money. I promise."

Nazia watched, amused at the exchange. The boy was clearly mocking baji for bringing a girl as her mazdoor. The bazaar was teeming with people, and nearly all carried their own baskets or employed the services of the Afghani boys. The fact that the baji did not casually call upon the services of one of the boys to hold her goods as she ambled from stall to stall, throwing hundred-rupee notes on mangoes the Afghani boys were not allowed to touch, was an obvious outward sign of the baji's depleted status: that she was one of the many in the posh area of Defence who could barely keep up the economic pretense of belonging in the upscale society so far removed from the poverty of Karachi.

"Fine," Seema said with a dismissive wave. "If you want to carry the baskets, go ahead. Nazia, give him everything."

Nazia bit her lip to keep from smiling and gratefully handed over the baskets containing the three-kilo sack of potatoes and two-kilo bag of turnips. The boy winked at her before pulling the handles of the woven baskets together and slinging them over his shoulder.

Now Nazia was able to carry the smaller items that Seema bought from the vendors who roamed the market, hawking their goods in bullhorn voices that carried far over the steady din of barters. Cilantro, mint, and gnarled gingerroot fit easily into her shoulder bag. Nazia pulled out the money Amma had given her and chose a handful of items after carefully watching Seema pick through a pile of tomatoes, discarding the rotten ones by tossing them toward the back. She moved on to the guava, holding the golden-green fruit up to her nose, sniffing for the sweet pungency that meant soft and ripe, but not so ripe that grubs had made the fruit their home.

By the time the grocery shopping was finished, Nazia's head was pounding from the heat and lack of breakfast. She longed to stop at the cold-drink stall, but her money was spent and she knew better than to ask baji. She breathed a sigh of relief when Seema turned toward the front of the bazaar, where their driver waited.

The boy followed behind them, doubled over, carrying the baskets like a donkey with satchels tied to both sides. Nazia felt a pang of guilt for carrying the smaller bags, even though they, too, weighed at least five kilos by this time. Seema baji carried nothing except for her own purse.

"Do you need any help?" Nazia asked.

The boy grunted and shook his head, watching his steps through a shag of hair that fell over his eyes.

Nazia kept moving, trying to keep the baji in sight. Seema was nearly at the edge of the bazaar, where the overhead tarp gave way to the scorching sun. Nazia hastened her steps, knowing that Seema would hate having to stand in the open field. As she moved forward, she felt her dupatta slither away from her shoulders.

Absently she reached up to keep it from falling but was met by a tug that ripped the cloth from her fingers. Shocked that the Afghani boy could be so bold, she turned to glare at him and give him a scolding, but was taken aback by the girl that stood before her.

"Saira!" She couldn't believe her eyes. "What are you doing here?" Nazia dropped her sack and flung her arms around the girl.

Almost immediately she felt Saira stiffen. Nazia squeezed her eyes shut for a moment, remembering that they had been friends since the age of five. She took that memory and locked it away before releasing Saira and stepping back with a painted-on smile.

Saira brushed a hand over her kameeze, absently wiping away any residue from the contact. "I'm shopping with my mother." She glanced at the Afghani boy loaded with goods. "What are you doing here, Nazia?"

Nazia cringed, too conscious of her threadbare clothes, her unwashed hair, and the purple half-moons under her eyes. "I'm here with . . ." Her voice caught. "I'm here with baji, the woman we live with," she mumbled, and looked away. In the distance she saw Seema beckoning to her, her mouth moving. Even the Afghani boy waited for her, and his back seemed to stoop lower and lower to the ground with every passing second.

"Are you her servant?" Saira finally asked.

Nazia's smile tightened. "Yes. It's working out really well, Saira.

I mean, we have a nice place to live in the best part of the city, and she treats us well and doesn't work us too hard."

"NAZIA!!" Seema was standing at the edge of the tent, waving furiously at her.

"I have to go," Nazia said. The mazdoor was making his way to the car with the baskets.

"Wait!" Saira called. She stepped forward but didn't touch Nazia. "We miss you at school. When the other kids ask about you, we tell them you went back to your village." Her cheeks reddened slightly. "We thought maybe you wouldn't want everyone to know that you are a house servant."

"I'm not just a house servant." Nazia's voice was brittle. "I'm a masi, too. I go door-to-door and clean the bathrooms and floors for rich people."

Saira's eyes widened. "We just thought that it would be better if the kids at school thought you went back to Punjab to get married."

"And what if I want to come to see you or Maleeha in Gizri? Everyone will know then that I am still here and never got married."

"We didn't want you to be, you know, ashamed about it."

"NAZIA!" Seema barreled toward her. "Come now or you walk!"

Nazia took one last look at her friend before walking away.

"Well, what were we supposed to say?" Saira shouted behind her.

Nazia walked swiftly past Seema, leaving just enough distance so the woman couldn't reach out and grab her. She mumbled an apology to the memsahib, who replied with a barrage of insults. Nazia tossed the remaining bags into the dickey and glanced back at the bazaar, but Saira was gone. The Afghani boy closed the trunk and jogged around the car to hold the door open for her.

Perhaps it is a good thing that we were interrupted, Nazia thought. She could still feel the way Saira had stiffened and tried to step back when they embraced.

She stowed herself in a corner of the backseat and stared out the window as the driver maneuvered the car around the small sand dunes that dotted the makeshift parking lot. The mazdoor had slapped the dickey as the car left, and she turned and waved through the back window. She wondered if Seema had paid him for carrying the bags.

The car stopped short at the gate. Before she could get out, Nazia heard the iron bolt slide from the shaft. She wondered if Abbu had come to visit. He was usually allowed to leave the construction site on Sundays to spend the day with his family before he had to head back with the sahib on Monday mornings. Maybe with Sherzad gone, Abbu would be allowed to remain at the house as their new gatekeeper. Perhaps if they all lived together, it would almost be like home.

Sherzad stood next to the gate. As the car passed by him, he raised his gaze to Nazia's and stared with hollow eyes. The skin around his cheeks was bruised and his lower lip was cut.

As soon as the car jerked to a halt, Nazia scrambled out and ran to the boy. She moved quickly, knowing she had only a few seconds before Seema would be beside her. The gate remained open for the neighbor's driver to return home after they unloaded the bags, but Sherzad had disappeared behind the mosquito netting of the chowkidar's room.

"Sherzad!" She shifted her weight from one foot to the other. "Sherzad, are you all right?" She waited barely a second before she flung aside the dingy netting, stepped into the shadowy room, and then froze when she came face-to-face with a woman who could only be Sherzad's mother.

The woman's piercing gaze bored through her like a knife. Nazia could almost feel her ransacking her thoughts, searching for the proof that it was she who had tricked her son into running away. After only a moment the woman lifted the corners of her mouth upward into a swarthy smile, revealing deeply stained large teeth. Behind her, Sherzad sat on the charpai, his arms wrapped tightly around his knees.

Nazia gasped as someone grabbed her shoulders from behind. Seema steered Nazia out of the room. "Go help with the bags. You've no business in here."

Nazia stumbled back into the sunlight and hurried to the car to gather a few of the bags from the dickey. The neighbor's driver sat languidly behind the wheel, not helping. Nazia huffed as she carried the larger basket of vegetables around the front of the house to the side entrance. She stopped to slip off her sandals before depositing the basket on the kitchen floor. She returned for the rest. She heard Isha and Amma call out to her, but she ignored them and hurried back. When she rounded the corner, she spotted Sherzad in the driveway and stumbled, stubbing her toes against the concrete. The skin scraped raw, but Nazia didn't feel the pain.

Instead she sucked in her breath sharply as she watched
Sherzad dance on his tiptoes while his mother pulled at his ear-
lobe, her elbow jutting skyward, her bangles clanking furiously
as she shook him like clothes drying on a line. Nazia stepped
back, stunned. What was the woman doing? Nazia could see the
memsahib standing on the other side of Sherzad, her hands on her
hips. But it was the high-pitched voice of Sherzad's mother that
carried across the yard and drew Nazia's mother and her siblings
from the veranda to huddle closer, where they could see what all
the wailing was about.

Amma watched in silence, then turned back to the veranda,
taking Mateen with her. "That woman has been here for hours
waiting to return the boy to baji," she called out to Nazia. "Surprised the child's still standing."

"What's wrong with her? Why is she so angry?"

"Parveen came here with fire in her belly when she thought
baji had replaced her son with us. She thought we had stolen his
duty. When I explained that baji had room for all of us and that
the boy ran away on his own, she went crazy. She couldn't believe
that he would bite the hand that feeds him and disobey her so
brazenly."

"Bite the hand that feeds him?" Nazia said sharply. "Sherzad's
mother doesn't feed him. He feeds himself by working hard for
everything he gets and doesn't get around here."

"I warned you to stay out of it, Nazia. He is just a child. Half the
pain that boy is suffering right now is your fault. For the beating
he is getting you are as much to blame, if not more. You live with
that, girl."

Nazia glanced down at Isha at her waist. What would she do if that were her sister out there? Would she be cowering behind the wall as she did now, waiting out the beating for a chance to offer condolences? Or would she have the courage to rush forth and stop the grossly unmatched assault?

Finally the memsahib pulled the boy away from his mother and wrapped a heavy arm around him. She laughed, telling his mother that was enough; did she mean to kill the poor boy? Nazia's mind did somersaults as she realized they were now reversing their roles, so the baji appeared kinder and more loving, offering relief from the pain his mother inflicted. The memsahib tousled the boy's shaggy hair, then hugged him close. Sherzad's mother was quiet now, and the baji's voice lowered to a soft murmur as she clucked inaudibly, soothing him.

Sickened, Nazia clutched her sister and walked numbly back to their quarters. She'd let Seema take in the rest of the bags. She would not touch them. Nazia was acutely aware of Isha's vicelike grip but did nothing to loosen the little girl's bony fingers.

The sound of snoring coming from the sleeping quarters confirmed that Abbu had returned home. Instead of collapsing on the adjacent charpai, Nazia carefully set the shopping bags on the ground just outside the door so as not to disturb him. She shuffled back to the kitchen and poured herself a tin cup full of water from the metal cooler on the counter. The chilled water was not normally meant for the servants, but Nazia didn't care. She was exhausted from the bazaar and knew that it would be at least another hour before the afternoon meal would be ready. She gulped down three cups before the memsahib returned with Sherzad.

While Seema heated up leftovers in silence, Nazia set about the task of cleaning the vegetables for storage. No mention was made of the boy's return or of the party the night before.

While Nazia stood at the sink rinsing mustard greens and spinach leaves, she snuck glances at Sherzad. If he knew she was watching him, he didn't show it. He knelt down stiffly to set a shallow pan of flour on the floor. Nazia stepped aside when he came to the sink to fill a glass with water, and then watched him carry it back to the pan. Slowly he poured the water at intervals and began kneading dough for the afternoon bread.

How can he go on as though nothing happened? What kind of boy would not cry after being turned away by his own mother? She watched his body sway back and forth while he pushed and pulled at the stiffening dough, his shoulders scrunched upward as he worked. At the stove Seema stirred the yellow lentils. Nazia realized the scene was the one she'd lived every day since moving into Seema's servant quarters. Nothing had changed, and only the bruises on the boy's face were different.

After lunch Nazia lay on the charpai, pressed between Amma and the wall. Abbu lay on the other bed, Mateen and Isha sprawled across him. It was late in the afternoon, and the house was locked up so the sahib and baji could nap. Sherzad slept in his room by the gate, his mother long gone after collecting his wages and food to return home with.

Abbu's voice — a steady, deep murmur that sounded like soft drums — rose and fell as he told stories about the men he met on the site, the building they were constructing, and the petty antics of laborers who plagued the project. His beard had grown long and was singed with gray. Deep grooves etched downward from both sides of his wide nose to the corners of his mouth. His lips were darker than before and cracked from constant exposure to the sun. His shoulders were still wide enough for Isha and Mateen to rest their heads, but his frame somehow seemed smaller.

Nazia lay on her side, leaning against her mother's ample back, the ropes of the charpai digging into her elbow as she listened, half sleeping, to the melody of her father's voice.

Abbu patted his left thigh with a heavy hand. "My leg cries every time I walk the boundary. Five times a day, after every Azan. The call to prayer is the unrelenting alarm clock that forces me to walk all four corners of the sahib's massive construction site." He shook his head. "Chowkidar, they said. A chowkidar sits at the gate and lets the public in or keeps them out. A man with a bad leg should sit at the gate. Not walk the boundary five times a day." Abbu muttered under his breath. He caught Nazia's gaze and said, "Tomorrow I will stay home with you. Tell the sahib in the morning that I am ill."

Nazia glanced down at her mother's closed eyes, then looked back at her father and nodded. He could rest for a few days, and with Sherzad's ordeal behind them, it was likely that the mem-sahib would let it slide.

"Good girl." Nazia cherished the warmth of Abbu's smile.

The following day a grumbling sahib drove away while Abbu slept past noon. Nazia cleaned the house alone, allowing her mother time to rest with Abbu. Since it was common for masis to miss work without calling, as most had no access to telephones, Nazia took advantage of this fact and skipped the other houses. *One day won't get me fired,* she thought. She supplemented the baji's sparse meal by digging out a few saved rupees to buy kebab rolls from the Defence Market. The pleasure on Abbu's face as he bit into the spicy meat and licked the dripping grease from his wrist made Nazia full. She'd even had spare notes to buy one for Sherzad, who accepted the treat with barely a nod.

Abbu stayed in their quarters for most of the day, except only when nature called, and even then he was careful to limp in case the baji was watching.

As she did every afternoon, Seema locked herself inside the house so she could take her afternoon nap without fear of intruders. Nazia was exhausted from doing all the cleaning and running to the market. Amma, Mateen, and Isha were already asleep, so she decided to lie down on the remaining charpai.

Although the slant of the sun proved that time had passed, it seemed as if only a few moments had gone by when the air was filled with Seema's shrill cries and her father's deep voice. Nazia awoke with a start, confused and groggy.

"What happened?" Amma asked, suddenly alert. Abbu's voice boomed from the front of the house, forcing Amma to sit up quickly. "Ya Allah," she muttered. "What has that man done now?" She swung her legs off the bed and sat up slowly. She winced and stood by degrees, the weight of her own body almost too much for her feet to bear. She walked barefoot with heavy steps to the door and pushed it open with her hip.

Nazia squinted as she watched her mother waddle along to the front of the house. Isha and Mateen were still asleep. She wanted to go back to sleep and let Amma tell her what had happened when she returned. But when Amma disappeared around the corner, the voices grew louder. Nazia's skin prickled despite the heat. What could have happened? When the air became charged with Amma's voice, high-pitched and pleading, Nazia stumbled out of the quarters, her curiosity transformed into a cold fear that spread across the back of her neck.

She ran around the house, down the sloping driveway, and outside the open gate. A peddler with his two-wheeled cart was parked under the shade of the neem tree. Abbu stood beside the cart, looking both belligerent and sheepish. The peddler and Amma were speaking over each other, vying for the baji's attention.

When Seema spotted Nazia, she snapped her fingers at her and called out sharply, "Go get Sherzad!"

Nazia ducked back into the driveway and rapped on the door to the gatekeeper's quarters. "Sherzad! Wake up, Sherzad!"

Nazia noticed that the door was slightly ajar, so she opened it farther, pushing aside the mosquito netting to meet the boy's steady gaze. "Baji wants you."

Sherzad rose calmly and came out into the street, where Seema ordered him to relieve the peddler's cart of his wares.

The peddler protested and pressed his palms together. "Baji, I bought these goods and have already paid your chowkidar." He nodded at Abbu. "You can take back the goods only if he gives me the money back."

"He never gave me any money!" Abbu shouted, shifting his

weight from one foot to the other. "I had only loaded the materials on the cart, and you came out before he paid me."

"Check his pockets, baji." The peddler wrung his hands together, twisting his fingers, locking and interlocking them. "You and your chowkidar are trying to rob a poor man who makes an honest living. You can't take back the merchandise *and* keep the money! How will I survive?"

Nazia looked at the cart more closely and recognized machinery, spare parts, and scrap metal—all the sahib's property that had been stored for so long in the back room adjacent to theirs.

Abbu was stealing! Nazia tasted metal and clenched her jaw to hold down the bile. Abbu must have quietly collected the items to sell to the scrap dealer while they all slept. Seema had probably heard or seen him carrying the materials to the gate. How else would she have known he was out here?

How could he do this to them? Nazia was dizzy with grief. Grief for herself, for her siblings, and for her mother. But most of all, grief over the knowledge that Amma was right about Abbu.

"Nazia! Don't just stand there. Help Sherzad move everything inside." Seema began lifting pieces of scrap metal off the cart and placing them in the driveway. She paused in front of Nazia's mother and said, "Get the money out of your husband's pockets, or you can leave with him right now." She brushed past Nazia and continued to carry the sahib's scraps back through the gate.

Amma berated Abbu and scuffled with him until she managed to pry the money from his kurta. Nazia's cheeks grew hot as she noticed the neighboring servants and chowkidars coming out to watch the spectacle.

Within minutes the machinery and metal parts were whisked back to the storage room and the scrap collector's money was returned. Seema snapped her fingers at Sherzad. "Go and get the other children." She turned back to Amma. "You can come and get your things when you've found some place else to stay."

Amma's eyes widened. "But baji, where will we go?" She grasped her arm. "Please, don't punish us all for my stupid husband's mistake."

Seema shook herself free. "He is useless now. How can we trust him? God knows what he's been doing at the sahib's site. Instead of guarding, he's probably been selling off the sahib's supplies and equipment, then blaming it on the laborers."

"I stole nothing. I swear to you." Abbu hung his head, but there was no conviction in his voice.

"Don't you speak to me," Seema said, her voice grim. "You get away from here and don't come back. Take your wretched family with you." She turned to Amma. "You've all been nothing but trouble since the moment you arrived. Take your children and get out. I have Sherzad. I don't need the rest of you."

"Baji, please," Amma whispered, her hands clasped together. "We have nowhere else to go."

Seema turned her gaze toward Sherzad, who stood at the gate. "Are you deaf? Go and get the children." Sherzad edged around the back of the house.

Amma suddenly collapsed at Seema's feet. She clutched Seema's ankles through her thin shalwar and looked up, her eyes pleading. "Baji. I will send Saleem away. When he finds work, he will call for us. Let us stay until then."

Nazia tried to lift her mother by the arm. "Amma, what are you doing? Get up." Her mother's flesh was hot as she twisted out of Nazia's grasp. "Amma! You don't have to do this. We can find another place." She gritted her teeth together to keep from shouting. "We don't have to beg. Stop begging!"

When Amma looked at her, Nazia recoiled at the desperation that glassed over her mother's eyes. The truth was painfully apparent. There really was no place else to go.

Behind her, Isha and Mateen whined as Sherzad led them through the gate and onto the street. Abbu was standing off to the side now, almost melting into the gathering crowd. Was he already washing his hands of them? It dawned on Nazia that Abbu would not stop Amma from begging. Nor would he beg in her place. He was going to take care of only himself, the way he always did. She felt as though a thick black blanket were descending over her, smothering her in heavy darkness. Why hadn't she seen it before?

She glanced around slowly until the crowd came into focus. There was no savior. No uncle, brother, or father would come and rescue them. They were all strangers. It was up to her and Amma to salvage what they could from Abbu's dreadful mistake. She turned away from Abbu and the rest of the onlookers and wiped her eyes until Seema was no longer a blurry vision of sweltering rage.

"Baji." Nazia lifted her chin. "What Abbu did was wrong. We have served you well, haven't we? Let us stay. I promise, we will not betray you."

Seema stepped back and tried to extract her leg from Amma's grip. "I won't listen to you, Nazia. Not this time."

With all the will she could muster, Nazia took a firm grip of Seema's wrist. "Yes, baji. Listen."

Seema pulled her wrist away and balked. "And why should I?"

Nazia bent down and slowly pulled Amma from Seema's feet. "We have no place to go. And because I am not my father. I am not a thief."

Seema sighed audibly. The crowd of onlookers on the street had grown, and they pressed forward, eager to hear the drama unfold. "What are you all looking at? Go on back to work!"

Seema waved her hands at them as though shooing gulls from a picnic on the beach. "Vultures feeding off the misery of each other, that's what you all are. Get away from my house!" She shoved a boy standing nearby, and slowly the crowd began to disperse, snickering as they left.

Abbu took a few more steps back when Seema gave him a withering look.

"Do you hear Nazia?" Seema shouted scornfully. "You do not deserve a daughter with such dignity. You allowed your wife and daughter to beg on your behalf. What a pity you are. At least one good thing has come of this."

Abbu stepped forward eagerly, as though forgiveness were a possibility. The baji held up her hand. "Not one more step. At least now your family knows your true colors." She turned to Nazia. "I don't know why I should listen to you, Nazia, but you can stay. If I ever see your father around here again, I will have him skinned alive."

"Thank you, baji. Abbu will leave immediately."

There was no word from Abbu, whether he had found work or not, and even Isha and Mateen did not ask when their father would return. November dragged along, and Nazia and her mother tended to their duties without protest, even when Seema asked that all the dust-infused rugs in the two-story house be washed and scrubbed by hand.

Ramadan was only a few weeks away, and the only respite from the heat came at night, when cooler winds blew in from the Arabian Sea. The vast ocean was only a stone's throw away, but Nazia still hadn't found the time to visit Clifton Beach.

One evening after dinner, when the dishes had been put away and Seema had gone to lie in bed to soothe a pulsing headache, Nazia sat on a bamboo chair outside their quarters, watching Isha and Mateen snuggle close to Amma on the charpai. Sherzad strolled the width of the house barefoot, from one boundary wall to the other, his hands clasped behind his back. After a while he pulled up a chair and sat down beside Nazia, his body sliding down to mold with the curve of the bamboo. He tipped his head back and stared at the night sky. "I've decided to leave," he said.

Nazia rolled her head to the side to see Sherzad better, but only his shadowy profile was visible in the dim light. "Again?" She watched his mouth curve up into a smile. When he didn't answer, she sighed. "Do you enjoy getting beaten?"

"I've learned not to listen to you." He chuckled. "I've learned not to go to my mother."

"Where will you go?"

"Back to the village. To my dadi's house in Punjab. To my grandmother."

"How do you know she won't send you back?"

"When I was little, I used to follow my dadi everywhere," he said. "She never sent me away. I would follow her around, and she would tell me stories as she worked. She'd sew little flowers on dupattas. Pink. Green. Blue. It was my job to separate the threads so they would fit into the eye of the needle. Sometimes she'd give me the needle and let me help. Every time I pulled the needle through, she'd say, '*Shabash*, beta, shabash.' Not once has my mother ever said 'Good job, child, good job.'"

How many times had Nazia heard her own mother say "shabash" to her? A thousand times. "Shabash, beta, shabash." It was a small word, but when the task was difficult, like when she first learned to roll out a perfectly circular roti and cook it on the *thawwa*, "shabash" had filled her with pride. Or when she had made her first shalwar kameeze for the doll that Abbu had bought her when she was nine. She made the outfit out of leftover scraps from the sewing Amma did, and when it was done, Amma had gone to the bazaar and bought new lace trim to tack onto the sleeves and the bottom of the kameeze. "Shabash, beta, shabash."

"What will you do there?" Nazia asked.

"I don't know. We have a school there. Or if Dadi wants me to help with other things, or put me to work there, I'll do that. Whatever she asks, so long as she lets me stay." He paused. "I need your help, Nazia."

Nazia shook her head. "I tried to help you before, and look what it got you. Beaten up, that's what. Even Amma warned me not to interfere, but I didn't listen." She touched his knee. "I'm sorry for the trouble I caused you. You were happy here before I came along and ruined things."

Sherzad scoffed. "I got in trouble plenty enough long before you showed up."

"That's not the point." Nazia wrapped her arms around herself. "The point is you were happy here doing what you were supposed to do. I'm sorry for taking that away from you."

Sherzad stood up swiftly. "How do you know I was happy? I was happy in Punjab—that's why I'm going back. I'm tired of moving around from one baji to the next. If I obey my mother, I will be a servant forever. If not for this baji, then someone else."

He looked over at the charpai where Isha and Mateen now lay sleeping with Amma. "Look at them. Your sister is no bigger than me. She does nothing all day because your amma refuses to allow her to work. She follows you around, begging to help because she doesn't know any better. But if she was forced to do it, would she still want to?"

His voice caught, and Nazia was certain that he was crying.

"Why can't my mother do that for me? I have many older brothers and sisters who work, so why must I? Why can't I just go to school and play cricket like other kids? It's not fair."

Nazia stood and gathered Sherzad in a hug, grateful when he didn't pull away. Why were some decisions so difficult to make, while others could be made in a heartbeat, so long as it was not *your* life? Sherzad's forehead pressed against her ribs as he wiped his eyes with her kameeze. She patted his knobby shoulders and wished that he were her brother. She would trade Bilal for this slip of a boy any day.

"I will help you," Nazia whispered. "I will help you go home to your dadi." If she could not escape so easily, then the least she could do was ensure Sherzad's freedom. The boy sniffled quietly and squeezed his thin arms around her, making it hard for Nazia to breathe. But she said nothing and stood there in the darkness for a long time comforting him, planning for him. This time she would get it right.

The next afternoon Sherzad slid the bolt out of its socket and lifted the door to keep it from squeaking. Nazia slipped out of the small opening.

"Now remember, if Amma asks where I am, tell her that I am in the house dusting. If she asks again, tell her baji sent me to the market to fetch some yogurt. Amma should not be a problem. Let her sleep as long as possible, and stall baji if she asks for me. Just don't let them know where I am." Nazia glanced quickly down the street, then back at Sherzad. "Keep Mateen and Isha occupied if they wake up. Don't let them disturb Amma."

"I know, I know." The day had heated up considerably, despite the cool breeze that had blown in the night before. Sherzad hopped from one foot to the other as he tried to keep the soles of his bare feet from burning on the concrete driveway. Despite his discomfort, he grinned and wiggled his eyebrows. "Don't get lost, and don't lose the money."

Nazia rolled her eyes at him. "Please. I know exactly what I'm doing." She didn't, of course, but there was no reason to worry him. "I'll be back as soon as I can. Less than two hours."

"Go now!"

Nazia wrapped her dupatta over her head and secured her sandals. She knotted a small plastic bag tightly, then threaded her arm through the handles so no one could snatch it away easily. She hurried off down the hill toward the bus stop at the edge of Defence Market. She crossed the main road, passed the mosque, and wove her way through the rows of shops that spread like serpents through the small valley. The aroma from the *botti* and kebab stalls made her mouth water, but she didn't dare stop. She had less than two hours to get to Gizri and back before Amma and Seema would know that she was gone.

She boarded the bus in front of the meat stall and chose a seat behind the driver, checking and rechecking her dupatta. Indian dance music reverberated throughout the bus. She kept her gaze fixed on the window behind an old woman clad in a long black *chadar*, careful to avoid anyone's curious stare. Although it wasn't unusual for a girl her age to take the bus alone, she didn't want to risk doing anything to draw attention to herself.

The ride was shorter than she expected, and she jumped off before the bus came to a full stop on Gizri Lane, just across from the market where she used to meander through the mishmash of stalls with Saira and Maleeha after school. *Let Maleeha still consider me a friend,* she thought. Clutching her bag tightly, she ran past the familiar dirt road alongside the cricket field. Nazia darted across the street as soon as a gap in the traffic opened up, and she headed straight for the Gizri School for Girls.

She walked down the hall, turning her head away as she ducked past the principal's office. She stopped short at Ms. Haroon's door and took a deep breath.

She knocked loudly on the door. A sea of faces bent studiously over the desks looked up in unison. Nazia tried to ignore the collective gasp that spread throughout the room, and focused only on Ms. Haroon, who sat at her desk fanning herself. "Um, Ms. Haroon?"

Ms. Haroon's hand paused in midair as recognition dawned on her. "Nazia?"

Nazia forced herself not to step farther into the room. She felt like a beggar standing there in her shabby outfit, while the rest of the students were wearing their crisp white uniforms. She tried to keep her voice firm. "I need to speak with Maleeha. It is very important."

Nazia fought back the urge to cry as her teacher glided toward her and ushered her back into the hallway. Ms. Haroon pulled her into a warm embrace. "Nazia," was all she said.

Nazia's eyes closed and she breathed in Ms. Haroon's perfume. She wondered if this was what the roses and pine trees from Shangri-la smelled like. Tears seeped into the corner of her mouth, and then she imagined she tasted fresh water from the river that flowed through the foothills in Sialkot.

"How have you been?" Ms. Haroon was smiling, but her eyes were serious.

Nazia pulled back. "Please," she said hurriedly as she averted her gaze. "I need to talk to Maleeha."

Ms. Haroon held on to Nazia's arms. "Maleeha has spoken to me about your family. If there is anything I can do for you, Nazia, you must let me know."

Nazia's throat squeezed closed and she could only nod.

"I mean it, beta. You are bright. I know your life has been difficult these past few months. But I feel strongly that you need to get off this path. It's not for you."

What was she saying?

"I know it seems as if there's no way out right now, with your family destitute," her teacher continued. "But you needn't be caught up in it. Whether you know it or not, you can choose. And I know you can choose a better path."

Nazia was mesmerized by these words, but what Ms. Haroon was suggesting was impossible. What could Nazia do except what she was already doing? What else existed?

"I don't know what else I can do. My family needs me. Amma needs me." Nazia stepped back and leaned into the doorway, scanning the room for Maleeha. She locked eyes with her friend, pleading silently.

"I'll be right back, Ms. Haroon," Maleeha called out to her teacher. "I forgot to mention that I was expecting Nazia. It's a family matter — it'll only take a moment."

Maleeha propelled Nazia down the hall, around the corner, and into the girls' bathroom. Maleeha hugged Nazia fiercely.

"I am so happy you are here. I missed you so much!"

Nazia tried to wiggle free. "My clothes. They're filthy. Stop it or you'll ruin your uniform."

Maleeha stared at her friend. "I don't care! I'm just so happy you came!" She pulled Nazia close again and spoke into her dupatta, her voice muffled. "When I didn't hear from you after I told your father where your family was staying, I wasn't sure what had happened to you. You know how hard it is for me to get away, and my mother wouldn't bring me to see you. I didn't know what to do." She stepped back, keeping hold of Nazia's free hand. "I knew that if I waited, you'd come sometime."

Nazia was startled by her friend's reaction. "But I thought you'd be busy with school, and with Saira. I met her at a Sunday bazaar. Did she tell you?"

"She said she thought she saw you, but that it was someone else."

"It was me. We spoke."

"Well, don't worry about it now. Saira has her own problems." Maleeha shook her head. "Now, tell me. What are you doing here? Is your father okay?"

"I haven't much time. I have a favor to ask of you. Are you willing to help me?"

"Of course! Just tell me what you need."

Nazia handed Maleeha the plastic bag. "There's money in here. Have your brother buy a one-way ticket to Multan. It's a long story, but it's for a little boy who is trying to get home. His mother offers no protection. If he stays with the baji, I am afraid for him. I'd buy the ticket myself, but you know how it is. Your

brother is older, and no one will question him." Remembering
that Saira had told her that everyone thought Nazia had gone back
to her old village, she continued, "Tell your brother the ticket is
for me, that Amma is sending me to live with relatives in Punjab,
but she doesn't have the time to go to the station to buy the ticket
because of her work. Tell him Abbu is already there."

"Don't worry; I'll have it done for you." Maleeha took the bag.
"But how will I get the ticket to you?"

"Remember the address I gave you? We are staying at the same
place. But ask Hisham to buy the ticket for next Sunday. I will
come back for it."

Maleeha nodded. "Okay. But if it's too hard for you to get away,
maybe I can ask Hisham to bring me to you."

Nazia shook her head quickly. The thought of Maleeha seeing
where she lived gave her goose bumps. She was certain Maleeha
would look past the upscale neighborhood and see only the small
servant quarters with the weathered charpai. "No. I'll find a way
to come back again." She squeezed Maleeha's hands. "You know
your mother will stop you, now that she knows I am a masi."

"No she wouldn't!"

"Hush! I have to go now." Nazia hugged her friend, then shook
the dupatta from her shoulders and wrapped it around her head.
When she was sure the hall was clear, she motioned to Maleeha
and stepped out of the bathroom. Maleeha followed behind her.
They gave each other one last kiss on the cheek and parted.

Nazia passed the principal's office, her sandals slapping loudly
against the gritty floor. She pushed open the heavy double doors
and was momentarily blinded by the intense sunlight. She shaded

her eyes as she scanned the busy road for signs of the bus back to
Defence. A bus on the other side of the road pulled to a stop in
front of the cricket pitch.

My bus! she thought. *I can't miss it!* She ran alongside the road,
then dashed across the street when she saw an opening. A horn
blared at her. She swerved off the road and scrambled to the berm,
where the coarse sand sprayed over her sandals and wedged itself
between her toes.

The bus began to pull away. "Wait!" She raised her arms and
waved wildly at the men who hung on to the back of the bus like
monkeys hanging from tree limbs. "Wait!" But she was too far.
Nazia watched in dismay as the bus moved away and disappeared
into the swell of traffic.

She was sure that Amma must be awake by now. And what if
Seema discovered Nazia was not in the house?

She backed away from the bus stop to the low stone wall
that bordered the front of the cricket pitch, and sank to the
ground. There was nothing to do but wait.

Nazia had thirty minutes to wait for the next bus, so even though it wasn't her usual pick-up time, she decided to stop by at the *darzi's* to pick up some sewing so she'd at least have some excuse for her absence. The darzi loaded her up with several kameezes and dupattas that needed repair or embellishing, which Nazia took gratefully. Now she had the excuse she needed for her disappearance, as well as a way to replenish her depleted funds.

She decided it was best to simply ring the buzzer when she got back. She heard the slap of sandals against the concrete driveway, then the clang of the bolt sliding from the socket. Sherzad peeked out. He squeezed through the narrow opening. "What took so long?"

"I missed the bus."

"The ticket? Did you get it?"

"Yes, yes. It's done. Maleeha's brother will take care of it."

Sherzad wrapped his arms around her waist, squeezing hard.

"Oh, stop it. If you want to thank me, take these bags."

He took the bulky plastic sacks of clothes, and Nazia shook out her arms to ease the numbness. "Do they know I'm gone?"

Sherzad balanced one bag on his head and the other on his hip. "No. That's the best part of all of this. Amma asked about you only a few moments ago when Seema baji wanted tea. I wasn't sure what to say, since they were both awake, but I remembered that you really only go out to get the sewing, so that's what I told them, that you went to the darzi." He grinned. "And you did!"

Suddenly Seema's sharp voice interrupted them. "Who's there?"

"Coming, baji, coming," Sherzad called out, carrying the bag of clothes as though it weighed as much as he did.

Nazia followed Sherzad through the gate and slid the iron bolt into place. Sherzad disappeared toward the back of the house, leaving her alone to face a congregation on the front lawn. Seema baji sat on a bamboo chair sipping her chai. Amma, Isha, and Mateen sat in a half circle on the dried grass not far from Seema's feet. Nazia was surprised to see that Amma was drinking tea as well, while the little ones were munching on cumin biscuits. And Amma's friend Shenaz sat on the ground beside Amma, her face streaked with tears. All heads turned when Nazia approached.

"Why didn't you tell me you were going to the darzi?" Seema demanded. "You could have brought the eggs and bread from the market."

"I'm sorry, baji," Nazia replied, contrite. "I didn't want to wake you."

Shenaz's guttural moan interrupted.

"What happened?" Nazia shook off her slippers and sat down close to Shenaz. "Why are you crying?" Gingerly she took a corner of the swarthy woman's dupatta and wiped away the tears that dripped down her leathery cheeks.

"I'm all alone in this world," Shenaz wailed. "I have no place to go. The world has forsaken me!"

"Please, Shenaz." Seema rolled her eyes. "Stop being so dramatic. Of course you have a place to go. Surely someone from your previous jobs can take you in."

"Everyone has forgotten old Shenaz! Baji, you are the only one who has let me pass through the gate."

Puzzled, Nazia looked at her mother.

"Shenaz's brother-in-law kicked her out," Amma explained.

"Why?"

"Why? Why?" Shenaz wailed. "Because he is a beast like all other men!"

"Children are listening, Shenaz. Hold your tongue." Amma glared at the weeping woman. "Isha, get up! Take Mateen with you and fetch a glass of water."

"Her brother-in-law accused her of stealing from him," Seema said. "So he turned her out."

"I did not steal!" Shenaz's voice was filled with venom. "He only wanted my sister to believe that."

"But why would he do that?" Nazia asked.

Amma scoffed. "*Chup!* You ask too many questions that are none of your concern. She's been accused of stealing; she was kicked out from her sister's house. That is all you need to know."

Nazia felt a stab of pity for Shenaz as she remembered how confident the woman had been when they had first met at the meat stall. She had been proud of her independence and her ability to come and go as she pleased. Now, it appeared, she was homeless. "What about your husband? Won't he take you in?"

"I've already tried. His other wife won't allow it."

Seema swatted at a mosquito on her leg. "Why don't you just go back to your village?"

Shenaz opened her palms. "Baji, you know I can't. They don't think well of me since my husband took another wife."

"I wish I could help you, but you know my house is full. I couldn't possibly feed another mouth, even if it's yours." Seema shook her head.

With Abbu gone, there was space for Shenaz, but Nazia knew the decision was Seema baji's to make. She tried to think of something to help the free-spirited woman who had helped them in their time of need. "What about Fatima baji? Have you gone to her?"

Shenaz turned to her. "No," Shenaz said, shaking her head slowly. "I forgot about her."

"Well, when we were looking for a place to stay, she offered to take me without the rest of my family. Of course, Amma wouldn't allow that. I know her chowkidar and his family returned to their village to work in the fields and they haven't come back yet. It wouldn't hurt to ask."

"Maybe. After all, I did bring you to her," she said, almost to herself. "Are you still cleaning for her?"

Nazia glanced at Seema and answered in a rush, "Yes, but it's almost too much with Seema baji's work, the other house on the street, and the sewing from the darzi. Amma helps, of course, but still, I do most of the work. I wouldn't mind giving Fatima's cleaning to you."

A nervous chuckle erupted from Amma. "Nazia, you don't

know what you're saying. Of course we need Fatima's work. How else will we rebuild your jahez?"

Nazia swatted the air with an impatient hand. "Amma, please stop worrying about the jahez. The wedding is off. There's no hurry."

"I am the mother of daughters. There is always a need to hurry."

The night of the party rushed back and swallowed her whole. Nazia was suddenly back on the charpai lying next to Sherzad gazing out at the stars through the opening in the tin roof of the chowkidar shack. All mothers were alike, Sherzad had said. All wanting to get rid of their daughters. Nazia knew in her heart that couldn't possibly be true. It didn't matter to Nazia what all mothers wanted to do with their daughters. Only what Amma wanted to do with her.

"Why, Amma? Why is there a need to hurry? What is it about daughters that makes mothers want to get rid of us?"

Amma exchanged glances with Seema and Shenaz and then laughed.

"Your innocence is your mother's responsibility," Seema explained.

"My *innocence*?" Nazia almost spat. "You mean the way I innocently used to go to school and learn my subjects without worrying about where we would sleep or where our next meal would come from? What's to protect? That innocence is gone."

"Don't talk back to the baji," Amma scolded. "Even if you no longer go to school and you earn money cleaning houses and sewing clothes, that doesn't mean you know the ways of the world. You've a lot yet to learn, beta."

Shenaz placed a bony hand on Nazia's leg. "I can see you are viewing the world differently since the last time we spoke. The contempt for the way I choose to live is no longer in your voice. Listen to your mother. She knows what she speaks of. Look at me. I thought living free would suit me. A lifetime later I am childless, and no one cares. I am husbandless — that is all the world sees. A woman without a husband is a woman less than worthless."

Nazia edged away from her. "How can you say that? You said you have loved the way you lived."

"Yes, but what does it matter if I end up living my old age out on the streets, a beggar no one can look in the eye?"

The words of the three women did somersaults in Nazia's mind. She knew only one thing for certain: Shenaz had helped them even when Nazia was unwilling to believe that it was what they needed at the time. "You may take Fatima's work or any of the other houses we have. You need it more than we do." Nazia stood and turned to her mother. "Don't worry, Amma," she said stiffly. "I'll bring more sewing or find another house to clean or something. You will get your jahez."

On Thursday the late-afternoon sun cast long shadows across the front lawn, where Nazia sat on the brittle grass trying to finish up the sewing. Using her teeth, she pulled out old thread from a blue kameeze, then proceeded to sew it up again to make the shirt five centimeters roomier.

As soon as the last of the sewing was complete, Nazia would

have the excuse she needed to venture out to the city and retrieve Sherzad's ticket. Sunday was only three days away, and she prayed that Maleeha had been able to convince her brother to go to the station.

As the needle dived in and out of the cloth, Nazia thought about Sherzad. From the moment the plan to escape was set in motion, he was a changed boy. He laughed at the slightest hint of amusement and even managed to make the memsahib explode with laughter at his hilarious antics. He zipped from task to task, barreling through the work as though he had the energy of four grown men. He didn't even complain about the small amount of food he was given or the stiffness of the tandoori bread that was always a day old.

Nazia couldn't help but be uplifted by the boy's crooked smile and the adoring way he looked at her. She only hoped that the plan would work, and that his dadi would welcome him home. She could get him on the train, but what happened when he got to his grandmother's—that was not in her control.

As Nazia finished the sewing, the buzzer rang.

Sherzad hurried out of his quarters. "Who is it?"

A muffled and high-pitched voice wafted over the iron gate. "Maleeha. I'm here to see Nazia."

Sherzad glanced at Nazia and opened the gate before she could stop him.

What was Maleeha doing here? Nazia stuffed the kameeze into the bag beside her and stood up. Before she could brush off the dust, Maleeha was through the gate, running toward her. Behind her, Hisham had stopped in the driveway to look around.

"Nazia!"

"What are you doing here, Maleeha?" Nazia laughed as she tried to keep her balance. "I told you I would come to you."

"I know, but I wanted to see where you lived. I don't often get to come to Defence." She shot her brother a look and dropped her voice. "I convinced Hisham to bring me. We told Amma we were going to Clifton Beach."

"Clifton Beach!" A stab of jealousy cut through Nazia. Clifton was practically within walking distance of Seema's house, but ever since they had started working here, they'd never managed to go. Before his accident Abbu had often taken the whole family to spend the day by the sea.

"We're still going," Maleeha said. "Amma asked us to bring her some roasted corn. Why don't you come with us?"

Nazia glanced at Hisham and suddenly felt awkward. He was one of the cricketers she'd watched year after year on the pitch in Gizri. "I can't. Did your brother go to the station? Did he buy the ticket?"

"Yes, yes." Maleeha pulled out a piece of white paper folded into a small rectangle and pressed it into Nazia's hands. "The ticket is inside. The Sunday trains were sold out, so he wasn't sure what you wanted him to do. Hisham said that since Sunday is everyone's day off, those trains are booked farther in advance. We only had a few days, so he got the last train out on Saturday night. It leaves at half past midnight."

"Saturday! But the baji is having another party that night. She'll expect us all to be there to help."

Maleeha shrugged. "You'll have to work that out with the boy.

Who knows? The party might be just the distraction for him to get away."

Just then Seema stepped out onto the porch and peered at the newcomers. "Sherzad! Who's come through the gate?"

Sherzad stood on the cement planter that bordered the driveway, separating it from the front lawn. He had been eagerly listening in on Nazia and Maleeha as they discussed his fate. "Nobody, baji. Just a friend of Nazia's."

"You know you're not supposed to let anyone inside without asking me first."

"Baji, it's just—"

"Baji, they are harmless." Nazia moved onto the driveway, where she could see Seema. "They're neighbors from Gizri. They just stopped by on their way to Clifton Beach."

Maleeha smiled. "We stopped to see if Nazia could come with us. We won't be gone long."

Seema studied the girl, taking in her tailored shalwar kameeze, the neatly braided hair, and the heeled sandals. Her eyes slid to Hisham, who was clad in denim jeans and a T-shirt emblazoned with Western logos.

"This is my brother," Maleeha said. "He'll make sure we're back before *Maghrib* prayers."

With an indifferent wave of her hand, Seema gave her consent. "Be sure to tell your mother where you are going so she doesn't worry about you again. And don't be long."

Nazia nodded. "Shukriya, baji." At least now she wouldn't be forced to entertain Maleeha and her brother in the servant quarters.

As Seema headed back into the house, Sherzad jumped off the planter wall and called after her. "Baji, can I go?" He clasped his hands together and threw in a flashy smile.

Seema whirled to glare at him. "Why don't you *all* go? I'll be the chowkidar!"

Muttering to himself, Sherzad disappeared inside his quarters. Before Seema could change her mind, Nazia went back to the servant quarters.

"Maleeha is here? Why didn't you tell me?" Amma struggled to lift herself from the sagging ropes of the charpai.

"Her brother brought her. They were on their way to the beach and just stopped to see if I can come with them. Seema baji said it was okay."

Amma straightened herself, causing her knees to crack. "Hisham?" The creases in her forehead deepened. "Does he have any news about Bilal?"

"No, Amma."

Amma pushed past her and headed to the gate. "You could have at least asked him for news of Bilal. What kind of sister are you?"

Nazia groaned and stomped after her mother, ignoring Sherzad's scowl as she passed the chowkidar's room. Outside the gate Maleeha and Hisham were already seated on their motorbike.

"Hisham!" Amma waved her arm frantically.

They exchanged perfunctory greetings before Amma launched into her questions about Bilal.

Hisham gave an indifferent shrug. "I haven't seen him."

Nazia knew that despite the fact that Hisham and Bilal were the same age, and had shared the same teachers and lived within shouting distance for so many years, they had never really been friends. The only times she could recall ever seeing them together were out on the cricket field.

"What about your friends? Someone must know what happened to him." Amma glared at the boy, her disappointment obvious. Nazia wondered how Amma could care about Bilal after all that had happened, but she knew there was no point in questioning her mother. Bilal was her eldest son, and Amma still held a sliver of hope out for him.

Hisham fiddled with the key and started the engine. "If I hear anything, I'll let you know," he said finally, before turning to Nazia. "Are you coming?"

She nodded and straddled the bike behind Maleeha. Nazia waved at Amma as they sputtered away, leaving her standing at the side of the road in a puff of dust.

The ride to the beach was short but exhilarating. Nazia scooted closer on the narrow seat and loosened her grip on Maleeha. The dipping sun spread a golden glow that blanketed the street and streamed through Maleeha's hair. Her sheer dupatta flapped in the wind, and Nazia held it down to keep it from whipping into her face.

Hisham expertly maneuvered the bike through the steady traffic, avoiding craters in the road. Each home they passed was an architectural feast for Nazia's eyes as she tried to imagine the kind of people who dwelled inside.

The more lavish homes had guards lounging outside the main

gates, staring at passersby. Although some wore uniforms and had rifles strapped to their backs, many wore simple kurtas, giving them the appearance of loiterers instead of guards.

As they came upon Clifton Beach, the massive homes gave way to more diminutive seaside apartments. The paint on the exterior walls was corroded from years of exposure. Hisham turned onto the main thoroughfare that ran alongside the ocean, and for the first time in months Nazia saw the full glory of the Arabian Sea.

Hisham passed the parked cars and found a spot to park by the seawall. Leaving Hisham to follow a few steps behind, Nazia grabbed Maleeha's arm and led her down the broad concrete steps to the sandy beach. She took off her sandals and carried them as she ran alongside Maleeha to the beckoning sea.

Maleeha splashed the hems of her pants as she came to a stop, the water up to her calves. "Look at Allah's work. Doesn't everything seem better when you come here?"

Gulls flew overhead, and miniature crabs scuttled at their feet. Nazia lifted her shalwar and walked slowly into the ocean, relishing the cold water lapping at her ankles. She dug her toes into the submerged sand and felt the granules lodge underneath her toenails. "It's wonderful." She looked out across the gray-blue water toward the fishing boats heading toward land. Far on the horizon she could see two navy ships signaling to each other with powerful lights. The sun was low, and the sky was streaked with purple and ink. She could feel Maleeha watching her.

"Things haven't been the same since you left," Maleeha said. "Let's walk, Nazia."

Nazia walked beside Maleeha, keeping her gaze down, taking

care not to step on the crabs or the decaying starfish that littered the sand.

"How long do you think you'll have to do this?"

Nazia shrugged. "Longer than Amma ever expected. Abbu was caught stealing from Seema, and she made him leave. No one knows where he is." She shot Maleeha a look. "Like father, like son, don't you think?"

Maleeha held Nazia's free hand, their fingers entwined, just as they used to do on the way to school when they were younger. "None of that is your fault," she said earnestly. "How long will you have to continue to pay for their mistakes? Don't you worry about the future?"

"How can you ask me that, Maleeha?" Nazia stopped walking. "Do you think I want to clean houses for the rest of my life?"

Maleeha let go of her hand. "What about school? You should at least finish your degree. Why can't your mother see that, especially with the marriage proposal finished?"

Nazia turned to look at the sea and continued walking. The light had faded fast, and the wind had picked up, bringing in colder air from the sea. She wrapped her arms around herself, her sandals still clutched in one hand. The towering spotlights installed intermittently along the seawall came on and illuminated the beach with an intense fluorescent glow. She glanced back and saw that Hisham was a few steps behind them, deliberately keeping his distance.

"Right now," said Nazia, "I'm the only person earning money for the family. Amma doesn't even come with me anymore to the other houses. I do those after lunch while Amma rests. She gets too tired, and her legs don't hold her up the way they used to. I worry what will happen to her if Seema ever turns us away." As she listened to herself say the words, she realized that she would be stuck cleaning houses and sewing clothes for a long time.

Maleeha tugged at Nazia's arm, forcing her to stop. "Maybe you don't have to do everything your family does. Maybe you can leave too, like your father and your brother. Maybe——"

"No," Nazia said vehemently. "I could never leave Amma, or Mateen and Isha. They need me."

Maleeha clucked her tongue. "I know they need you. But you need to think of yourself, too. If you stay with your mother, you *will* be spending the rest of your life cleaning houses."

"But what can I do?" Nazia looked at her friend, exasperated. "Leaving my family is impossible!"

"What if I told you there was another way? What if I told you Ms. Haroon would take you in? She would make certain you finished school."

Ms. Haroon? When she wasn't teaching, she was traveling all over the world. She'd never have time for someone like Nazia. And even if she did, that was a dream more impossible than being Fatima baji's house servant!

Nazia turned away miserably. Maybe Abbu and Bilal could leave so easily, but Nazia knew she could not. Caring for her family, being loyal to Amma, these were duties ingrained within her and could not be changed so easily. How would Amma manage? Who would help with Isha and Mateen? She felt queasy. No. Leaving Amma was impossible.

The girls stared out at the ocean. After several minutes Maleeha said, "Just think about it. That's all I ask. Okay?"

Nazia bit her lip. She couldn't say yes to something she knew was not possible.

Maleeha groaned. "Fine. You still have your books, don't you?" Nazia nodded.

Maleeha bounced lightly on her toes as she formulated a new plan. "What if I brought you the class assignments and you did them on your own? After my papers are graded, I'll bring them and check your work. At least that way you won't fall so far behind in school."

"Why would you want to do that?"

Maleeha stopped bouncing. "Because we always did everything together, and I told you, things just haven't been the same since you left."

"What's wrong, Maleeha? What could possibly be different? You still have Saira."

Maleeha threw her up her hands. "That's just it! You're gone and Saira's changed. She's just not the same anymore. Her abbu got some government posting, and she's been acting snotty ever since. We don't eat lunch together anymore because she's made friends with Leila and her group. The only time we spend together is on our way to school and back. And she only does that because we live on the same street." Maleeha shook her head. "I don't know. She hasn't really said anything, but I know something is different."

Nazia recalled the way Saira had recoiled when Nazia hugged her at the Sunday bazaar. There had been something different then, but Nazia had thought that it was because she herself looked so scraggly. "Don't let her upset you. I will always be your friend, no matter what happens to me or you. Now, about those books."

"You're the best friend ever!" Maleeha cried.

Nazia hugged her friend and resolved to keep their friendship intact and to keep up with her studies. Finding spare time in the evenings would not be a problem. After the dinner dishes were done, Seema usually left them alone for the rest of the evening. Fighting fatigue would be her main concern. She would find the strength. "Do you think Ms. Haroon will let me take the annual exam? Do you think she'll let me pass?"

"I don't see why not. They should let you take the exam if you've prepared for it. But even if they don't, it doesn't matter. At least you will know the lessons and can keep up with me. And then you can stop cleaning and find something better."

Nazia suddenly realized that she *did* have a choice. Amma could stop her from going to school, but she couldn't stop her from learning her lessons. "Fine," she said in a whisper. "If you're willing to help me, how can I not?"

"We'd better get going," Maleeha said. "My mother is probably furious at me for being gone so long."

"And Hisham is a saint for bringing you." As they turned back, Nazia asked, "Do you think your brother knows anything about Bilal?"

"I don't think so. They weren't really friends, were they?"

Nazia shook her head. "It's just hard not knowing. Sometimes I forget I have an older brother too. Your parents must be pleased Hisham's going to college."

"He's working, too, paying for it himself." Maleeha waved to her brother, and he turned and started back for the seawall.

When they walked up the stairs to the parking area, Hisham veered off to buy coal-roasted corn from a stall nearby. Maleeha moved toward the bike and freed a bag strapped into the rear basket. She pulled out shiny pink chiffon. Even with the night settling in and the fluorescent glow of the spotlights casting stark shadows around them, Nazia knew instantly that it was the same material they had seen that day at the market. In her mind Nazia could see Maleeha standing at the edge of the cricket pitch wearing this exact same outfit not too long ago. It was beautiful in the market, and it was even more exquisite on Maleeha.

"I brought it for you. I want you to have it," Maleeha said softly.

Nazia was so grateful, she didn't even have the heart to protest. Getting this gift from Maleeha was far more meaningful to her than any of the outdated hand-me-downs Seema had given to her. Nazia searched her friend's face and found not even the faintest hint of pity. "Thank you."

Hisham returned with enough roasted corn for all of them. Nazia carefully placed the clothes back in the bag and secured it in the basket. She took her corn smothered in lemon juice, salt, and ground chili peppers and bit into it, suddenly ravenous. She gave a silent prayer, grateful that her friend had opened her eyes to all the possibilities that lay before her, and that none of them included cleaning houses. *Shukriya, Allah,* she thought. *Shukriya.*

As the hour of Sherzad's secret departure neared, preparations for the party pressed on. To Nazia's dismay, it was not to be a simple dinner party. It was a celebration of the completion and sale of the sahib's latest construction project, a soap factory. Nazia overheard Seema baji talking on the telephone, saying that the sale of the soap factory would finally bring the sahib back to the level of success he had enjoyed before his finances had been sabotaged by bad contracts. Nazia hoped that the sahib's success would mean the baji would finally pay her and Amma for their labor even though the agreement was only for room and board.

News of the factory's completion charged Seema with an excitement that Nazia had not witnessed in the months she had been employed by the baji. The baji's nervous energy permeated the house and drew everyone into the task of cleaning and preparing for the party.

For the next two days Nazia, Amma, Sherzad, and even Isha scrubbed the house down, dusted, washed, and swept until their shoulders felt weighted with cinder blocks and their gaits took on decidedly noticeable limps. Even Shenaz, who'd found a job two doors down, moonlighted to help weed the garden, beat the

silt-infused rugs, and scrub the layers of packed dust off the dete-
riorating metal window screens.

Nazia went to bed exhausted, too tired to discuss Sherzad's
escape plans with him. His ticket was hidden in her bag of soiled
clothes, the bag itself stuffed in a corner of the servant quarters
behind the charpai she shared with Isha. She could only hope that
once he got off the train at Multan, he'd know how to find his way
to his grandmother's house. She guessed that he'd been dreaming
about his escape for so long, for her even to worry that Sherzad
might get lost was simply ridiculous. He could probably find his
dadi blindfolded, with his ankles strapped together. Sherzad was
the only one who went to bed each night with energy left to spare
and secret thoughts that kept his eyes open far into the night.

On Saturday the caterers came just after four o'clock to set up
the tent. They brought stacks of red chairs with foam backing and
lined them in rows facing the house. As the workers began setting
up the tables and chairs, Nazia went inside to make the afternoon
tea. While the kettle simmered, she peeked through the window
curtains in the dining room to watch the flurry of activity at the
front of the house. Sherzad fussed with the chairs while the other
workers set up tables in the driveway for the serving area. Cooking stations were set up for a chicken tikka barbecue and a pit for
the naan, which would be freshly baked.

The double doors of the wrought-iron gate were wide open,
with the back end of the caterer's truck partially in the driveway,
the front end jutting out into the street. Neighboring servants
and chowkidars milled about, murmuring among themselves and
craning their necks while they tried to see inside.

When she heard the whistle of the kettle, Nazia went back to the kitchen and removed it from the stove. As she stood on her tiptoes and reached for the cups, the kitchen door squealed. Sherzad stood at the screen door, his expression worrisome.

"What's wrong?"

"Your mother wants you out front. Your abbu is here."

"Abbu?" Nazia set the cup down with a bang. She wiped her hands on her dupatta and followed Sherzad.

She caught a glimpse of Amma just outside the gate. She couldn't tell if Amma was crying or laughing. A few workers peered curiously past the truck blocking the gate. Nazia ignored the workmen; she moved past the tables in the driveway and around the truck and stopped just outside the gate, where she spotted Abbu.

Her back stiffened. She called out her salaam without moving.

"What's this? No hug?" Abbu laughed. He came toward Nazia and hugged her. Her face was lost in his shirt, and the stench of sweat was overpowering.

"Look at you! What happened to you?" He pushed her away to take a better look. "You've grown so much. You're taller than your mother."

Maybe if you were around more, it wouldn't be such a surprise, she wanted to say. Instead she shrugged.

From behind Abbu came a gravelly voice. "The last time I saw you, Nazia, you were sickly looking. Your face is fresher now, and your father is right. You have grown."

Nazia stiffened as Abbu stepped aside, revealing Uncle Tariq. Nazia nearly gasped when she saw the man next to her uncle, a man Amma was clinging to now. The features that were always nothing more than a blur in her mind sharpened with sudden clarity as she recognized the boy she had once known as a child. The boy she'd once been engaged to. Salman.

What was he doing here? Nazia's heart started to race as she tried to fathom the meaning of the unexpected visit.

Amma released Salman's arm and waddled up to Nazia, her expression gleeful. "Your abbu went back to the village after the misunderstanding with baji. Tariq bhai was kind enough to take him in."

"Misunderstanding, Amma? Abbu was trying to hawk the things he'd stolen. You pulled the money from his pocket, remember?"

"Shh!" Amma glanced at Uncle Tariq. "Lower your voice, Nazia."

Abbu cleared his throat and leaned in closer. "We spoke of you and Salman," he said. "Your futures have been tied together for years. Angry words from old men should not change the course of destiny." He raised a hand to smooth his daughter's hair, but when she leaned away, he let it drop. "Your uncle has come a long way for you. Again."

Even before her father said the words she knew were coming, Nazia's knees trembled.

Abbu peered into her face, his forehead rippled. "I brought your uncle to prove to you that I fixed everything. He is willing to dismiss the jahez and uphold the engagement. Tariq and Salman are here to take you home." His brows lifted and his eyes shone. "Do you understand, Nazia? You're getting married!"

Nazia expelled her breath sharply. She turned toward Salman and noticed he wasn't much taller than herself. His frame was

much smaller and wider than Uncle Tariq's, and his belly pro-
truded, stretching his kurta. His face was weathered, but his
doughy cheeks and sagging chin softened the lines around his
eager eyes.

Could this be the answer to everything? No more cleaning
houses. No more sewing clothes for other girls. No more threadbare castoffs and hand-me-downs. Most importantly, no more
watered-down lentils and stale bread.

The sudden swish of a broom sliced through the heavy silence.
She saw Sherzad sweeping the already clean driveway, his body
bent at the waist, his arm moving in spastic jerks. His hair fell
forward in his face, so that Nazia could not see his eyes. But it was
obvious to her that he had overheard her father's news.

If she left now, how could she help Sherzad escape? With only
one servant on hand, Seema would keep the boy so busy, he would
never get the chance to sneak away and make it to the station in
time to catch the after-midnight train to Multan. How could she
give the boy so much hope, only to snatch it all away at the end?
But could she risk angering Uncle Tariq? If she refused to leave
now, would Uncle Tariq understand, or would he feel slighted
again? Would it mean that her chance to get married and return
to Punjab to live as Salman's bride would be gone forever? She
knew that her uncle's renewed offer of marriage was a magnani-
mous gesture, and one not to be taken lightly.

But something hard inside her, a stiffness she had not felt
before, kept her back straight and eyes defiant. She turned away
from Sherzad and found her cousin digging wax from his ears. His
mouth curved into a crooked smile while he extracted a pudgy

finger from his ear and wiped it onto the bottom of his kurta. Nazia's skin crawled.

She turned to her father. "I have to get back, Abbu. We can talk after baji's party."

Abbu shook his head. "You don't have to. You can leave with us this very minute."

Nazia tried to keep her voice even. "I can't leave now. Baji needs me."

"Don't be crazy, beta." Amma pressed her arm. "Seema will be fine. You gather your things and let's go."

"Amma, I can't."

"Why not?"

She knew her mother wouldn't understand. "If we leave now, Seema will be so upset, she'll make sure we never find work in the city again."

"Stop being ridiculous. After you get married, you'll never need to work in Karachi. There is no need to be so loyal. She is nothing to us. Let's get your things." Amma tugged Nazia gently.

"Nahi, Amma." Why was her mother being so stubborn? "Amma, I need time to think about this." She paused. "I don't know if I want to go at all."

"Are you mad?" Amma whispered. "This is what I have prayed for! Your abbu has finally done what he should and fixed the mess he started. Are you going to throw it all away?"

"No, I just—"

"Do you want to clean houses for the rest of your life? Do you want to end up like Shenaz?"

Nazia pulled her arm away. "No, I don't. But I don't know if I want to marry Salman either."

Amma gasped. "Ya Allah! I always knew you would do this!"

"Do what?"

"I've always told you that your thoughts were dangerous. Remember? Not those of a girl about to be married?"

"Yes," Nazia said. "But Amma, if you know this about me, why do you keep insisting I go against my wishes or my own thoughts? Why do you pray for something I pray against?"

Amma raised her hands. "Ya Allah, I should have paid attention to the signs. Why did you keep me blind? Ya Allah, grant me the patience to deal with this child," she cried. "Why are you doing this to me, ya Allah?"

Nazia glanced quickly at her uncle. "Amma, stop it," she hissed. "We have to make them leave!"

Uncle Tariq stepped closer, his mustache twitching. "What is this?" he demanded. "Is the girl rejecting my son?"

Amma and Abbu both turned to him, hastily assuring him that everything was fine. "Of course not! She's just confused about her loyalties," Amma said. "She is worried about the memsahib's party. Many people are coming, and Nazia feels badly about leaving now."

Uncle Tariq cast a stern look at Nazia. "She knows her responsibilities. She has never shirked them, even when her own father and brother have. Let her stay. We do not leave until tomorrow night anyway. Salman and I will come back for her on the way to the station." He called out to his son. "Is that fine, Salman?"

Nazia's cousin shook his head. "Why? We have only one day in

Karachi to finish the shopping. Nazia should come now to choose what she likes, and I won't have to listen to her complain about my choices after the wedding."

"I will be happy with whatever you choose," Nazia said. "Please go on without me and don't even think about my preferences. I'm sure you and Uncle Tariq have excellent taste. I couldn't possibly gather all my things and leave so abruptly. Please understand. One night. That's all I ask."

"All right," Uncle Tariq said finally. "Your father will come with us and choose on your behalf. We will return for you tomorrow evening before we leave for the station. Make certain you are ready to leave then, beta. There will be no more opportunities after this."

Nazia's shoulders sagged with relief. "Thank you." She backed away from her parents and her uncle, ignoring her cousin's scowl. *"Allah-hafiz!"* She walked through the gate and around the catering truck. As she passed Sherzad, he snapped to attention, tossed the broom against his shoulder like a rifle, and saluted her.

"You'd better be worth all this trouble," she muttered to him.

Sherzad laughed, and the sound lifted Nazia's spirits. She would do this one thing for Sherzad, and then she'd have to decide about her own future. She had less than twenty-four hours to make up her mind. *One thing at a time,* she said to herself. *First, free Sherzad. Second, free yourself, if you dare.* Nazia tried to push the nagging thoughts from her mind and rushed back to the kitchen, where the tea had turned cold and bitter.

Before leaving with his brother, Abbu had pulled Amma aside and demanded that Nazia be ready to leave tomorrow evening. Amma assured him that not only would Nazia be packed and ready to leave, but Amma and the rest of her children would also be ready to travel and attend the wedding.

Abbu planned to accompany Tariq and his nephew to the market, then return later in the evening in hopes of indulging in the deliciously extravagant food that would be left over from the dinner party.

Now, several hours later, Nazia sat on the veranda, exhausted. The party had started hours ago, and an endless procession of guests had passed through the gates, all eager to wish the sahib well on the successful completion of his soap factory. Sherzad had been planted at the gate, and there had been no chance to speak or prepare for his departure. Once the guests had arrived, he was assigned the task of ensuring the drivers and guards milling outside the gate received meals and drinks. He ran back and forth from the kitchen to the gate, fulfilling endless requests for more water, more bread, and more curry.

The din on the lawn, of people talking and laughing, of forks colliding against plates, and bottles of carbonated beverages jostling in their crates as guests sorted through the empty ones, gave Nazia a headache. Her arms ached from carrying trays of dessert plates and teacups to the ladies in the house.

When Abbu returned, she managed to convince one of the younger waiters to give her a plate laden with beef curry, chicken tikka, and spiced rice. She carried the plate and a bottle of cola outside the gate, where Abbu sat against the boundary wall.

Abbu took the plate eagerly. "Thank you, beta." Using his fingers, he shoveled the food into his mouth. When Nazia turned to leave, he grunted at her. "Wait." He swallowed a piece of beef without bothering to chew it and looked up into his daughter's face. "You are a lucky girl, Nazia. It is not often that a man gives the girl's family a second chance. Your uncle Tariq is my brother, I know, but even the bond that ties relatives together is a delicate one, easily broken."

"I know, Abbu." Nazia nodded absently.

"I am proud of you, Nazia. I am proud of the way you left school to help your mother when she needed you, the way you earn money to feed your family, and I am proud that you were compelled to stay to help the memsahib with her party."

"Thank you." The glow she usually felt when Abbu showered her with praise was gone. Instead a hollowness spread within her.

"But now it is time for you to get married. Don't let the rest of these worldly demands interfere and keep you from fulfilling your obligation to your parents and to Salman. He is a good man, and you will both be happy together."

"Will I get to finish school once I am married?" The question was out before she could stop it. But she had a right to know, didn't she? What if marrying Salman was nothing more than exchanging one form of servitude for another?

Abbu snorted. "Well, that would be up to your husband. Of course, there will be no need to finish school once you are married. I'm sure there will be plenty of work to keep you busy as you set up your new home. Decorating and all that."

"Salman has his own house?"

"Well, no, of course not. You will stay with his parents, as is customary. But I'm sure you'll want to add your own touches to the house, to make it feel more like home."

What touches? The home belonged to her aunt, her future mother-in-law. It was a well-known fact that every new bride deferred to her mother-in-law in all matters, from clothing to decorating. After everything she'd been through, did her father really think she cared about decorating? "I have to get back, Abbu. If you need more food, just ask one of the waiters. No one will mind."

"Thank you, beta. Don't forget what I said, now. Tomorrow when my brother comes for us, you should be ready to go. No excuses. Understand?"

"Yes, Abbu." Nazia left her father to go back inside. Sherzad stopped her at the gate and pulled her into the chowkidar's room.

"It's getting late. I've packed a small sack to take to the station. Is it time to go yet?"

Even in the darkness Nazia could see that he was bouncing, barely able to contain his excitement. "Almost. Let me go check the time. The train doesn't leave until twelve thirty, but you need time to get to the platform. Do you have everything you need?"

He nodded.

"Are you sure? You remember how to get to your dadi's house, don't you? If only you knew the address, I would feel so much better. You'll just have to let your instincts guide you, I guess."

"Don't worry, Nazia baji. I know Multan. I've traveled alone many times. It'll be easy to find her house."

Nazia wasn't so sure. He was still only a boy. But a brave one, she had to admit. What other ten-year-old would have the courage to escape by train in the middle of the night? She wasn't sure if even she could do it. *We all have our own challenges,* she thought. *The escape is his, the marriage mine.* "Gather your things, then. I'll be back with your ticket."

Nazia stepped out of the room and gasped as she collided into her father. His steel plate clattered to the ground, and she swooped down to pick it up. Had he heard her talking with Sherzad? Did he know what they were planning? She straightened and searched his face, but Abbu gave away nothing. "What are you doing inside the gate? You know Seema baji will have a fit if she sees you."

Abbu smiled. "I know. There are so many people, she probably won't even know I am here. Unless someone tells her, of course. I just wanted to get some more food."

"Go back outside. I'll get it for you." Nazia went back to the rear of the house, where the large pots of rice and curry were stored. She handed the plate to the cook, who ladled another serving onto it. "Do you know what time it is?"

The cook shouted to a passing waiter. Seconds later he said, "Ten o'clock."

Nazia gasped. Already? It would take nearly an hour to get to the station by bus. How could she have let the time slip away so quickly? She mentally kicked herself for not sending Sherzad off sooner. "Could you hold on to the plate? I'll be right back for it."

She went to her room, tore open the plastic bag, and rummaged through the clothes until her fingers touched the paper ticket. She wrapped the ticket in a fold of her dupatta, and clutching it tightly, she went back for her father's plate. With the ticket concealed in one hand and Abbu's plate in the other, she headed back to the main gate.

The chowkidar's quarters were empty and the gate was open. Nazia stepped out onto the road, where cars were scattered along the curb. Abbu was sitting on the hood of a car, talking to Sherzad.

"Abbu!" she called, and at the sound of her voice he slipped off the car and came toward her. "Your food." She handed him the plate. "You shouldn't be so obvious about being here. Later we'll try to sneak you in so you can sleep on the charpai, but in the meantime please try to stay out of sight. You know very well how the memsahib feels about you, and if the sahib knew you were here, who knows how he would react."

Abbu laughed. "You worry too much. The sahib always loved my work. It is your baji who is so hardheaded. Don't worry about me. I'll slip into the shadows here under the neem tree." He sauntered off toward the cluster of lean trees near the boundary wall.

Nazia turned to Sherzad. "We haven't much time." She unfolded the end of her dupatta and removed the ticket. "Put this in your bag and don't lose it."

Sherzad took the ticket, ran back into the chowkidar's room, and returned with his belongings to give her one last hug. "I will never forget everything you've done for me. You are the best sister anyone could wish for."

Nazia blinked to keep the sting out of her eyes. "Go now. When you get to the station, present your ticket at the counter and tell them your parents are sending you to Multan to stay with relatives. When you get on the platform, find some women to sit close to. That way no one will bother you. Go now. There isn't much time."

Sherzad stepped back. "I'll miss you. Remember to sleep where you can see the stars, baji. No matter what you've been through, the lights in the night sky will always soothe away the day's pain."

Nazia smiled. "So you're a *shahir* now? Stop stalling, poet. Go!"

Sherzad wove between the rows of parked cars, bobbing and bouncing as he went, before finally melting into the night.

Nazia whispered a prayer. Her task was done. All she could do was believe that he would make it home to Multan. She sighed and turned back to go inside. She would have to make sure that Seema baji didn't notice the boy's absence, at least until the train left.

Abbu was not at the wall, but his empty plate was. She picked it up and headed back inside. Feeling drained as she passed Sherzad's room, she was shocked to see a large foot hanging over the charpai. She stepped inside, and even in the darkness she knew it was Abbu. "What are you doing in here?"

He waved a hand at her. "I'm not hurting anyone. I'm tired. You've no idea how hard I've worked to coddle my brother's ego for you. Let me rest, beta. We both know Sherzad won't need the bed tonight."

Stiffly she backed out of the room. "Sleep, Abbu. I won't tell anyone you are here."

The next hour passed in a flurry of activity as Nazia struggled to complete her chores as well as Sherzad's. She cleaned up after the guests and corralled their children into one area of the yard. The dishes were whisked away by the catering company, and the tea station was set up on the front veranda. Surprisingly, the men from the catering company completed the tasks that usually fell on her shoulders, and she was genuinely glad for the sahib. His soap factory had made it possible to hire the catering company and ease her workload, and for that she was grateful.

The guests slowly departed, until only a few stragglers remained to chat with the sahib and sip tea in the drawing room. Nazia washed the excess kitchen dishes and utensils that had somehow found their way into the hands of the guests. When the buzzer to the front gate rang, Nazia dropped a serving spoon into the dingy water and prepared to go to the screen door.

At that moment Seema entered the kitchen. "Oh, leave it, Sherzad's there. He'll get it." She settled a tray of water glasses on the island. "Here. Wash these, will you?"

Nazia hesitated. If the buzzer rang again, then Seema would probably go to the gate to scold Sherzad for being so slow, and she would know he was gone. Quietly she turned away from the door. When the buzzer didn't sound again, she began washing the glasses. Maybe the caterers had left the gate open.

After the dishes were done, Nazia pulled out her steel plate and drinking glass. Finally she would eat. The caterers had carried the leftovers into the kitchen for the baji, who had drained the trays of beef korma and chicken tikka into her own pots for storage. Nazia moved to the doorway that divided the kitchen and the main lounge. She found Seema sitting on the settee with another guest, drinking tea and reliving the events of the evening.

"Baji gee."

"What is it now?"

Nazia lifted the plate. "I haven't eaten yet."

Seema sighed dramatically. "I'm too exhausted to serve you. It's all there in the kitchen. Take it out yourself."

Seema's friend turned to Seema and wrinkled her nose. "You'd let her do that? She might contaminate the rest of the food. You'd have to throw it all out then."

"You're right." Seema struggled to her feet. "That's the trouble with servants. You have to be vigilant all the time."

Nazia followed Seema into the kitchen. Fuming at the woman's humiliating comments, she held out her plate while Seema filled it with food. Her indignation slipped away as the aroma of spiced rice and beef curry caused her mouth to water. "Thank you, baji."

With a cup of water in one hand and her plate of food in the other, she moved toward the screen door. Now she wanted nothing more than to sit on the charpai in her room and eat her meal slowly, relishing each and every bite. She had made certain that her family had eaten earlier. Amma had finished her tasks and was lounging in the servant quarters with Mateen and Isha. Nazia was sure that her mother was unaware Abbu had returned. She wanted to keep it that way for as long as possible so that Seema would not catch wind of his presence.

As she was about to push open the door with her hip, the screen suddenly flew open and a thin woman barreled up the steps, a black chadar billowing behind her. Nazia gasped as she was shoved back against the cupboards and the food splattered across the floor at Seema's feet. Shouts rose up from Seema and the woman, while Nazia got on her knees to sop up her ruined dinner.

"What insolence is this?" shouted Seema.

The woman ignored the mess and clutched Seema's sleeve. An eerie wail escaped from the woman's lips. "Ya Allah! My son! What have you done with my son?"

Nazia looked up at the woman. The chadar slipped away and trailed behind her. The woman's face was contorted in anguish as she pleaded with Seema. It was Parveen, Sherzad's mother! Dazed, Nazia wiped up the food.

"You told me you were having a party when the sahib's factory was finished. I came to share in your happiness and pray for his success. You are always generous, baji, and I thought I would come and eat with my son. But what do I find? You have sent him away! He is gone!"

Seema pushed her away. "What are you ranting about? I haven't sent him anywhere. He's been here all night." Seema lifted her chin toward Nazia. "Ask her. They've both helped me tonight."

Parveen whirled at Nazia. "*Her?* This is all her fault! She's filled my boy's head with lies so that she could steal his duty and give it to her father."

Nazia stumbled backward until the marble edge of the counter pushed against the small of her back.

"Don't be ridiculous." Seema shook her head. "You always have this thing in your head that I'm going to replace Sherzad. He's a willful boy, but he does good work. Don't worry about it."

Sherzad's mother shrieked and pointed a bony finger at Nazia. "If he is so good, then why is her father in my son's bed? And where is Sherzad?"

"Baji, Abbu is here for only a few hours," Nazia explained. "His train leaves tomorrow. He just stopped to see Amma and the little ones."

"You meddling girl!" Parveen wiped spit from her mouth with her bare arm. "You are nothing more than a troublemaker, and I will make you pay if Sherzad has run away."

"I don't know where he is. I'm sure he must be around here somewhere. Maybe — maybe he went to the market."

"Liar!" Parveen shoved her hands against Nazia. "You don't fool me. From the first day I saw you, I knew you were the one who had filled my son's head with useless thoughts. If he is here, bring him to me now." Parveen turned back to Seema. "See, baji, what a conniving little fox you have working for you?"

"Where is Sherzad?" Seema glared at Nazia.

"I don't know."

"Has he run away again?"

"I — I don't know," Nazia stammered.

Seema's palm landed squarely on Nazia's cheek. "You must know something, or you wouldn't have dared to bring your father inside my walls. Speak up!"

Nazia cringed in pain as she cupped her face with both hands and ducked away from Seema and the crazed woman. She couldn't tell them about Sherzad and risk ruining his only chance for escape. There was no way she would let this woman find him. She guessed that at least an hour and a half had passed since Sherzad had gone. That meant that the train had not left and there was still a chance that he could be stopped. "I'm sure he went to the bazaar," Nazia said. "One of the drivers must have sent him. He'll be back soon."

Parveen sneered at her. "She is stalling, baji. She knows exactly where Sherzad is. I'm sure of it."

"Chup!" Seema pushed Nazia toward the kitchen door. "I want your father, that thief, out of here now. If the sahib finds him here, I don't know what he'll do to him. How dare your father come back here?"

Nazia stumbled down the steps and stopped short when she saw Amma hurrying toward her.

"What has happened?" Amma asked anxiously.

Before Nazia could reply, Seema and Sherzad's mother rushed outside and propelled Nazia toward the front of the house. "Don't worry, Amma," Nazia called out. The last thing she needed was for Amma to get involved and tell the memsahib that they, too, were leaving tomorrow for good.

Abbu was pacing in the driveway outside the chowkidar's room. When he spotted Seema, he stopped. "As salam-o-alaikum, baji." He put his hands together in a nervous greeting.

Seema swung the gate open. "Get out!"

Abbu cocked his head and attempted a smile. "Baji, why do

you treat me so badly? I don't deserve this from you. I'm sure the sahib would treat me better than you do."

"If the sahib knew you were here, he'd shoot you. How dare you come back to my house?"

"My family is here, baji. You would like me to give up my family?"

Nazia begged. "Abbu, please! Don't say anything. You'll only upset the baji more. Go to Uncle Tariq and stay the night with him. We will see you tomorrow."

"Have you told your baji you are leaving?" Abbu asked.

Nazia squeezed her father's arm. He had to stop talking! "No, Abbu. Not yet."

Seema gaped at Nazia. "What? You're leaving too?"

"I haven't decided yet, baji," said Nazia.

Abbu nudged her roughly. "What do you mean you haven't decided? There is nothing for you to decide. It is done. You leave tomorrow. Isn't that right, Naseem?"

Nazia turned abruptly, surprised to find her mother standing behind her. Amma crossed her arms and pressed her lips together, but her expression remained worried.

"Abbu, please, you must go now," Nazia pleaded.

"You weren't going to tell me!" Seema bellowed. "After I've treated you and your family so well, this is how you treat me? No notice, no warning, just get up and leave in the middle of the night like cowards? Is that what Sherzad has done? Answer me!"

"I don't know where he is," she said, her voice weak.

"I know where he is," said Abbu.

Nazia stared at her father. He wouldn't dare tell! Would he?

"Where is my baby?" Sherzad's mother cried.

"Abbu, go now," Nazia pleaded. "You've said enough."

Parveen snickered. "See, baji, she even knows how to silence her own father. What a gem of a girl."

A surge of energy rushed through Nazia's veins, and she whirled around to glare at the woman. "Stop it! Sherzad is *not* your baby. You treat him like chattel. You are the worst mother in the world. You don't deserve to find him!"

"Aha! So he *has* run away." She gripped Abbu's forearm. "You know where he is. Help a poor mother find her son."

"Of course." Abbu patted her hand.

Nazia gasped. "No, Abbu, don't!"

"I will tell you," he said, his voice even, "but for a price."

"Bartering on a child? You are worse than the devil himself." The woman dug her nails into Abbu's arm.

"Augh!" Abbu shoved her away. "Stupid woman. I know exactly where your son is, and there is still time to stop him." He turned to Seema. "You must understand, my daughter is getting married. Although my brother has not demanded a dowry, it would still be nice to have some money to offer the groom. Don't you agree, baji?"

"Humph. Once a thief, always a thief. Now a blackmailer, too, I see. Don't fall under his spell, Parveen. Your son is probably on his way to your own home, just like the last time."

Nazia twisted her dupatta around her hand until the circulation was nearly cut off. She realized that her father was willing to give up Sherzad for a few rupees. How could he do that, after all the planning and the waiting? How could he dash the little boy's dreams so easily?

"You should go home, Parveen baji," Nazia said nervously. "I'm sure Sherzad is already there. He just missed you and wanted to be with you, that's all."

"Shut up! I don't trust anything that comes from your mouth." She moved closer to Seema. "Please, baji. Give this man something, anything. I've worked so hard to raise my children. I have so many mouths to feed; I cannot suffer the loss of another income. When I find Sherzad, I will explain his duties to him so that he will not dare leave again. Please, baji, I need my son!"

After a long moment Seema finally spoke to Abbu. "Fine. Tell us, and I will give you the money Sherzad earned this month."

"But, baji — " Parveen recoiled.

Seema silenced her with an icy stare. "That is my offer. You people are all the same. Bartering your families for money and dowry. If you get your son back, then you can spare the loss of one month's income."

Nazia begged Amma to stop Abbu, but Amma seemed frozen, her eyes distant. When she realized that her mother would not speak up, she grabbed Abbu by the arm. "Abbu, why are you doing this? She doesn't care about her son. She only wants the money he earns. Don't you understand? I know you aren't like her. We don't need the money. Why do you want to hurt the boy like this? You don't even know him."

Abbu tried to push her away. "I'm not hurting him. I'm helping him. You have no idea what you have done. You're just a girl. And he is only a child, as small as Isha. Do you really believe he will make it? If we don't send someone now to get him, he will likely be mugged, or beaten, or kidnapped, or killed!"

A wail rose up from Parveen.

"Don't say that!" Nazia let go of her father's arm. "He is smart and brave. Children travel alone all the time in Karachi and no one thinks twice about it. Especially the poor. He is invisible. You're only saying that to get more money, because that's all you care about. Money! Not me, not Amma, not Isha, Mateen, or even Bilal. You are no better than Sherzad's mother!"

The impact of her father's hand on her cheek sent her sprawling. Her palms scraped against the concrete driveway as she tried to stop her slide into the planters that separated the lawn from the driveway. At once she heard a jumble of voices and shouting around her. Nazia recognized her mother and allowed herself to be lifted just in time to hear her father betray her.

"Sherzad left for the train station. He has a ticket for the twelve-thirty train to Multan."

The sahib's car roared away, leaving a cloud of dust in the deserted street. Only two cars and the catering truck remained. Abbu pulled the gate closed, not bothering to look at Nazia.

Nazia stared through the top rails of the black iron gate and prayed that the earth would swallow the sahib's car whole. Or that a truck accident along the way would bring traffic to a halt. Or that Parveen would be kidnapped at gunpoint. Anything to stop Sherzad's mother from reaching the station.

The guests remaining in the house trickled out and left the party, oblivious to the commotion. The waiters, who had melted into the background during the argument, came forward and quietly began removing the chairs from the lawn and stacking them into the truck.

Nazia allowed Amma to guide her back to the servant quarters, where Isha and Mateen were huddled together. She climbed onto the charpai and pulled Isha close. Mateen wrapped himself around Amma's legs.

"Have you eaten?" Amma finally asked.

Nazia was silent.

"I'll get you something." She placed Mateen on the charpai and headed to the kitchen. He immediately squeezed himself into a crevice between Isha and Nazia.

Amma returned with a plate of leftover chicken tikka, curry, and rice. "Take this. No sense in not eating."

When Nazia didn't move, Amma sighed and sat down on the edge of the charpai. The ropes creaked under her weight. Using her fingers, she squeezed at a piece of chicken tikka until the meat tore away from the bone. She buried the meat inside a ball of curried rice and then brought the mixture up to Nazia's mouth.

Nazia turned her face away. Amma moved her hand closer, and the aroma of the curry taunted Nazia's growling belly. How could she eat without knowing if Sherzad was safe? It was nearly midnight. She pushed her mother's hand away.

"Starving won't do the boy any good," Amma said.

Rage bubbled up inside of Nazia and burst from her throat. "You didn't do him any good either."

"Why should I?" Amma asked tiredly. "He is not my son."

"He's not Abbu's, either. Why did Abbu have to destroy Sherzad's only chance of escape? Why couldn't he keep quiet? Sherzad never did anything to him."

Amma lowered her gaze as she studiously molded bite-size balls of rice and chicken on the aluminum plate. "He's not destroying the boy's life," she said finally. "He's looking out for yours."

"How?" Nazia's voice was brittle. "By blackmailing baji to get Sherzad's hard-earned money?"

"Have you saved any dowry?"

Nazia groaned. "That again, Amma? I'm so tired of hearing

about the stupid dowry. I had some money saved. But I spent it on Sherzad's ticket. Thanks to Abbu, now even that is wasted."

"You bought his ticket?"

When Nazia didn't reply, Amma's hand stilled. "I knew you were involved. Didn't I tell you not to interfere with the boy and his mother? You have no idea what it's like to be a masi's child. Their lives are so different from ours."

"Aren't I a masi's child?" Nazia flinched when she saw the pain in her mother's eyes.

"Now, yes. But you weren't raised that way. I loved you and protected you, as I did all my children. Some masis are incapable of doing that. Their children are nothing more than another source of income to them."

"Isn't that what I am to you? Isn't that why you pulled me out of school to work?"

Amma's voice softened. "If that was the case, why would I insist that you marry Salman? I want you to have a settled future, not clean houses for the rest of your life."

"But . . . ," Nazia began.

"Go on and say it. Holding back from me will only make it worse for you later. It's better that you speak now, when only we can hear you."

"Fine," Nazia said, and she paused, choosing her words carefully. "What if marrying Salman is no different from cleaning houses?"

Amma set the plate aside and wiped her fingers on a rag. "I know Allah gave you a better brain to think things through with." She leaned back on the charpai and pulled Mateen up to lie beside her.

Nazia continued. "What if I spend all my life taking care of

Salman's house, his mother's house? Abbu said I probably won't be allowed to finish school after the wedding."

"That's your home too. It's your duty to care for your own."

"But what if I want to finish school? No one has asked me what I want. Not you, not Abbu, not Uncle Tariq, and not even Salman."

Amma chuckled. "Since when do we ask you? You've always known your fate was tied to Salman's."

"Are you going to slap me too, if I ask you how that is any different from the way Sherzad's mother treats him?"

"No. I won't slap you. But it breaks my heart to know you throw me in the same pot as her. I saved every year of your life for the day you would get married. That counts for nothing?"

"The dowry? Are you talking about the dowry again? Amma! Do you know who stole your precious dowry?" Somehow, almost miraculously, Nazia managed to silence herself. If Amma ever learned that her own son had stolen the dowry she had worked so hard to save, Nazia was certain, the knowledge would break her. "Nothing, Amma. Never mind."

Amma lay back and closed her eyes. Mateen snuggled close, and soon he was sound asleep. Nazia sat in the dim light of the servant quarters and stared at Amma. After a while Amma opened her eyes. She stared at the corrugated metal sheet that served as their ceiling.

"I know," Amma said. "I've always known."

"Know what?"

"I know Bilal emptied my suitcases, just as I know he hides from me."

Nazia stiffened. How could Amma know? "What?"

"He knows how hard I worked to save for your dowry. It is the shame of what he has done that keeps him far away."

"All this time you knew?"

Amma nodded.

Nazia's throat tightened, and her words came out in a croak. "Did you see him? Did he say something?"

"No. I haven't seen him since before your abbu got hurt. But the suitcase was not torn open. He used the key. The key I gave him to hold and protect for you. There was no other key."

Nazia's grip tightened around Isha's arms. When her sister complained, she lifted the girl from her lap and set her on the charpai. Her thoughts raced as she tried to think back to the day the dowry was stolen. Had she even noticed the lock was intact or the bag had not been cut? "Anyone could have picked that lock."

"But why would anyone else want to? Why was only our house broken into and no one else's? Stop. You know as well as I do it was Bilal."

Nazia twisted a loose thread of her dupatta around her finger. So much for protecting her mother. "I'm sorry you know. You shouldn't have to bear this knowledge about your son."

Amma's eyes remained fixed on the ceiling. "A mother always knows. Even without seeing, she knows. I know what each one of my children is capable of. I know their destinies long before they do. Before you do. But one day Bilal will have to come back."

"It's been months, Amma, and there's been no word. What makes you think he'll come back?"

"When? I don't know. But he'll return before he dies. Just as every child returns. He will come when he is tired and broken.

He will seek forgiveness." Amma's voice was strong. "He knows just as all children know that the gates of heaven lie beneath their mothers' feet. The gates of heaven are closed to Bilal until he repents for what he's done."

Nazia slumped back against the wall, Prophet Muhammad's (S.A.W.) famous words rushing up from the farthest corners of her memory, retold by mothers the world over, ingrained since birth.

"Why didn't you tell me you knew?"

Amma looked at Nazia. "Because I didn't know that you already knew."

"Maleeha saw him," Nazia admitted. "I made her swear not to tell anyone."

"Hmm."

"Why didn't you tell Abbu?"

"Because Bilal is like his father. Why do you think I work as a masi? Because it was all I could do to protect Bilal from his father. They are the same. No matter how much they mean well, they cannot fight the *shaitan* — the devil — that lives within. They know what is right, what is wrong, but they always do what they know best. Cheat. Lie. Steal."

"You think all of Abbu's family is like that?"

"All the men in his family. It's in their blood."

"Then why do you want me to marry Salman?"

"Of all the choices you have, I believe that is the best one. You're just a girl, Nazia. No parent wishes her daughter to be a servant or a street girl. You are better than that."

"I've gone to school. I know I could find something better,

Amma." She thought of Ms. Haroon. "There are other possibilities in life besides servant, wife, or street girl."

"You know nothing of this world, beta. Your dreams are like the rains. They may come for a day or two and fill you with happiness, but even the rain clouds must give way to the burning heat of the sun. Why? Because the sun rules this part of the world. Your dreams of school are nothing more than teardrops in a desert.

"What makes you think a girl like you could be someone, when your brother, a boy with a degree, couldn't even find a job selling newspapers on the roundabout? It's time you opened your eyes, beta, and learned the ways of the world. You must accept that marriage is the only way to protect you from the daily struggles that no female here could ever fight alone."

They sat quietly, and Nazia watched her mother drift off to sleep. She picked up the plate and ate cold lumps of rice balled together with bits of chicken. As she chewed the sticky mixture, she wondered if she would ever have the strength to make the sacrifices and choices Amma had made. She finished the food and stretched out beside Isha. She left the door of the servant quarters wide open so the sound of the main gate would reach her when the sahib and Seema returned.

Her thoughts swam together as she lay thinking of how much her life and her family had changed in the past few months. She wondered whether, if Abbu's accident never had happened, she would still be at home in Gizri, asleep on the floor next to Isha. Would Bilal be with them? There was no way to be certain, but still the thoughts lingered even when the blare of a horn erupted in the night.

They were back. Nazia moved stiffly off the charpai, careful not
to disturb her mother and siblings. Barefoot, she crept from the
room, squeezing through the narrow opening without touching
the door. As she hurried toward the front of the house, she heard
the iron gate swing open and the car sputter into the driveway.
At the edge of the house she peered past the hanging leaves of the
rubber tree and the jasmine shrubs that rose up to the banister of
the veranda. Was Sherzad in the car? Was his mother with him?

Seema and the sahib were alone. They entered through the front
door without speaking a word. Nazia watched for a moment
longer, then retreated while Abbu closed the gate. What did
this mean? Why was Seema letting her father stay? Where was
Sherzad's mother? Had Parveen caught the boy at the station
and taken him home? Or had the train already left when they
had arrived at the platform? The uncertainty twisted itself in her
stomach.

The idea of waiting until morning to know Sherzad's fate made
her gag. She clutched her stomach and pressed a hand against
the wall of the house until the heaving was done. Depleted, she
stumbled to the outdoor basin, where the dishes and laundry
were done. She rinsed her mouth and splashed cold water on her
face, then dried it with the bottom of her kameeze.

She sat on her haunches at the rim of the basin, her face buried in the stained cloth. Tears soaked her kameeze and seeped
through to her palms. Did she cry for Sherzad's capture or his
freedom? There was no was way of knowing, but she remained

by the rusty faucet until her shoulders stopped shaking and her calves ached from bearing her own weight.

When there were no more tears left, she wiped her nose with her shirt and struggled to her feet. She walked numbly back to her room and crawled onto the charpai.

Dim light from the neighbor's house slipped through the crooked wooden slats of the door. Did Salman's bedroom have windows? She tried to think back to the last time she had been to Uncle Tariq's house, but it was too long ago. The home was south of Lahore, in a small village set far back in the fields. The house had two rooms besides the main sitting area, and the meals were cooked outside. After the wedding would she get her own room, or would they put a mattress on the floor for her?

They would come for her tomorrow.

Nazia turned toward her mother, only to find Amma awake, watching her. Nazia drank in her mother's face, securing the precious image for when she was alone, when she would need it the most.

Nazia prayed silently for Allah to take care of Isha and Mateen, and especially Amma. She asked Allah to forgive her for what she was about to do, and she hoped that Amma wouldn't think she was abandoning her in the same way Bilal had. When the time came, Nazia wanted the gates of heaven to be open for her.

Nazia went outside to the basin and washed herself before performing the last prayers of the day. She knew the time for the final namaz was over, but she wrapped a scarf around her head, stood facing Mecca, and offered the prayers anyway.

When she was done, she returned to the charpai and kissed

Isha's forehead. She hoped lines of worry would never crease her sister's young skin. Gingerly she took off her scarf and covered her sister's feet. While Amma watched, she kissed Mateen, then gathered her belongings into a plastic bag. There wasn't much — only a few ragged shalwar suits and the precious pink chiffon outfit Maleeha had given her.

When Nazia was done, she turned back to Amma. Tears streaked her mother's face.

"Don't cry, Amma."

"I am afraid for you." Amma's shoulders shook.

"But you know why I do this, don't you?"

Amma rubbed her face.

Nazia set her bag on the ground and knelt down. She grabbed hold of her mother's feet. "Please forgive me, Amma. If I don't leave now, I will die slowly, softly, in a house that is not meant for me. I can't bear to be Salman's wife and spend the rest of my life stifling my own heart."

Amma covered Nazia's hands with hers as she struggled to speak without crying. "I know that, beta. I saw the vision long before it came to you."

"If you knew . . . all this time . . . why didn't you help me to understand?"

"Because the path you choose is a difficult one. One that no girl can ever find happiness in."

"It is the path my heart chooses for me. And true happiness can only come when the heart is free."

"I always thought that if I trained you well, taught you how to be an obedient daughter, one day you would make a good wife."

"One day I will," Nazia said. "Just not now. Not with my cousin." She squeezed her mother's feet. "Besides, it is you who taught me to make my own path."

"How?" Amma shook her head. "How have I steered you wrong?"

"You don't know if any of our choices are wrong or right, Amma. Your intentions were good, and that is all that's ever mattered. You decided to seek work instead of letting us starve. You made choices for us when Abbu didn't. Now I must make a choice for myself."

"Where will you go, beta?"

She thought again of Ms. Haroon and her offer to help. She remembered her conversation with Maleeha on the beach. She had played those words in her mind over and over as she had struggled to find the strength to leave her family behind. "Maleeha said that Ms. Haroon will take me in. That is where I'll begin."

Amma only nodded, and the silence stretched out between them. "You say that with such certainty," she said finally.

Nazia lifted her chin and puffed out her chest, the same way Sherzad had done that day they first met. "I have never been so sure of anything in my life."

Amma touched Nazia's lips. Suddenly she shifted her weight and moved clumsily off the charpai.

"What are you doing, Amma?"

"I've told you and I've tried to warn you. I know my children better than they know themselves." Amma rummaged at the back of the servant quarters, rifling through her belongings. From the folds of a chadar she pulled out a small purse made of blue silk.

"What is that?" Nazia leaned forward.

Amma sat down on the charpai next to Nazia. "This is for you," she said finally.

Nazia stared at the silken bag in her palms. She set the purse in her lap and carefully loosened the strings. She peered inside and gasped.

Nazia pulled out a thick roll of bills. All hundreds and five hundreds, and even a few thousand-rupee notes.

"I knew this day would come," Amma said. "I'd hoped and prayed it would not. But of course Allah's will rules over mine. He made you strong willed for a reason. He gave you thoughts that are usually reserved for men. He gave you wisdom that others were denied. Who knows why? We cannot fight it or deny it anymore, now, can we?"

Nazia held up the rupees. "But how?"

Amma waved a dismissive hand at the bundle of money. "You are destined to follow your own heart, not mine. Maleeha's mother kept it safe for me, for you, all this time. When we left Gizri, she gave it back to me, just in case we needed to spend it. But I never did. I suppose I always knew that you would need it someday."

"But this is so much money! You could have easily used it to replace the dowry."

Amma nodded. "I know. But by then a part of me already knew that marriage to your cousin was not your destiny."

"Then, why did you push it?"

"I had to try, didn't I?" Amma said, exasperated. "I've told you already — you have not chosen an easy path. But with every second that goes by, my insides are filling up with a peace denied.

I know I am doing the right thing now. And you will be happy, I promise you that."

Nazia sank against her mother in a tight embrace. *Shukriya, Allah, shukriya! Thank you, thank you!*

"Now, you keep these things safe here under the bed and sleep with me on the charpai for one last night. I am the one who took you from Ms. Haroon and brought you here. I will take you back to her myself." Amma gave Nazia's braid a gentle tug.

Nazia pulled back and wrung her hands as her elation turned to worry. "I don't want to cause you any more trouble with Abbu and Uncle Tariq. What would happen if they knew you helped me? And what if they try to stop me in the morning? Uncle Tariq will force me on the train!"

Amma carefully tucked the purse into Nazia's plastic bag and slid it under her charpai. "It makes no difference, beta, for you will always have my protection. I won't allow you to go like a thief in the night. You will hold your head up high and walk in the bright sun toward your destiny. And everyone will know that you have my blessings but not my fate. Do not worry about the men. I will make things right with them."

Amma motioned to Nazia. "Come, beta. May Allah watch over us all."

Nazia lay down beside her mother. The scent of coconut and mustard oil wrapped around them, and she allowed herself to be lulled by the achingly familiar fragrance. She breathed it in deeply so that when she slept alone, in Ms. Haroon's apartment in Karachi or her bungalow in the northern hills of Islamabad, Amma would be right there with her.

Amma's scent mingled with her own excitement, filling Nazia's lungs and stretching out her belly. She stared up at the stars through the tear in the roof and licked her lips. She tasted her own sweat and salt from the sea. For the first time in months she felt full.

URDU VOCABULARY LIST

abbu — father

Allah-hafiz! — literally means "May Allah protect you!" This is a
common greeting often used among Pakistanis for "Good-bye."

amma — mother

As salam-o-alaikum. — literally means "Peace be upon you."
Muslims say these words when they greet each other.

Azan — the Islamic call to prayer

baji — older sister; also often used to refer to any older female
as big sister, as a sign of respect

beta — generally refers to a male child or son, but is commonly
used across genders to refer to one's child

beti — daughter or female child

botti — small piece of meat as found in curry or stew

bhai — brother; also used to refer to an older brother or any
male of the same age or older as a sign of respect

biryani — Basmati rice with spiced meat, layered; served on
special occasions

chadar — oversized rectangular scarf used as a covering by
women for modesty

chappals — slippers or sandals; also may be spelled *chappalen*

charpai — bed of jute rope strung tightly across a wooden frame

chokri — slang for a girl

chotti — little one; generally refers to a girl child

chowkidar — gatekeeper

Chup! — Be quiet!

daal — lentils cooked to a soupy consistency

dadi — paternal grandmother

darzi — tailor

dickey — slang term refering to the rear or trunk of a car

dupatta — long, gauzy material draped over the shoulders, often
   used as a head covering

ghee — clarified butter

gosht salan — stewlike meat curry often made with tomato and
   onion base

haveli — a large country home

hijab — head scarf

jahez — the dowry a family saves for a daughter's wedding

Khabarnama — daily evening news program

kameeze — long, loose shirt worn by women or men

kayari — a flower bed or vegetable bed within a garden

kurta — long, loose shirt worn by men

lassi — yogurt smoothie

Maghrib — the compulsory daily prayer at sunset

mali — gardener

masi — woman who cleans houses for a living

mazdoor — person who performs heavy labor

memsahib — formal title for the lady of the house

naan — leavened flatbread

nahi — no

namaz — prayer

neem tree — tropical tree in the mahogany family known for its medicinal purposes

parratha — flatbread fried in ghee

qorma — meat curry richer than the everyday meat salan; generally reserved for special occasions

raita — yogurt sauce often including minced onions, cilantro, or mint

roti — thin, unleavened flatbread

S. A. W. — short for "Sallallahau Allahi wa sallam," which means "May the blessings and the peace of Allah be upon him." Muslims are required to say this after uttering Prophet Muhammad's name.

sahib — formal title for the man of the house

salaam — greeting

sarkar — landlord; man of the house

Shabash — Well done, or Good job

shaitan — devil

shalwar — loose, pajama-like pants worn with a kameeze

shahir — poet; also often spelled *shayar*

shukriya — thank you

thawwa — round, flat cast-iron pan often used for making roti, parratha, or other foods

tikka — grilled meat; can refer to chicken, beef, or any other type of meat

tonga — two-wheeled passenger cart pulled by a donkey

Uttoh! — Get up!

Wa laikum as salam. — May peace be upon you too. This is the reply to the greeting "As salam-o-alaikum."

wazu — ritual cleansing performed prior to daily prayers;
    also pronounced as "wadu" in Arabic

Ya Allah! — Oh Allah!

Zohar — second of five obligatory prayers